Barbara Steiner

OLIVER DIBBS
and the
DINOSAUR CAUSE

Illustrated by
Eileen Christelow

FOUR WINDS PRESS
New York

To those creative and dedicated teachers
in our schools who never get
the publicity they deserve.

Thanks to Ruth Sawdo and her fourth-grade students at McElwain
Elementary School, Denver, Colorado, who worked very hard on
Senate Bill 270—Stegosaurus for State Fossil. My inspiration for
Oliver Dibbs and the Dinosaur Cause came from one of the students,
who wrote to me, asking for my support of the bill.

Text copyright © 1986 by Barbara Steiner
Illustrations copyright © 1986 by Eileen Christelow
All rights reserved. No part of this book may be reproduced or transmitted
in any form or by any means, electronic or mechanical, including photocopying,
recording, or by any information storage and retrieval system, without
permission in writing from the Publisher.
Four Winds Press, Macmillan Publishing Company
866 Third Avenue, New York, NY 10022   Collier Macmillan Canada, Inc.
First Edition   Printed in the United States of America

10 9 8 7 6 5 4 3 2 1

The text of this book is set in 12 pt. Berkeley Old Style Book.
The illustrations are rendered in pencil.

Library of Congress Cataloging-in-Publication Data
Steiner, Barbara A.   Oliver Dibbs and the dinosaur cause.
Summary: Immersed in studying his favorite topic, dinosaurs, Oliver
involves his fifth grade class in a campaign to make the stegosaurus the
Colorado state fossil and runs afoul of an interfering bully.
[1. Dinosaurs—Fiction.   2. Schools—Fiction.   3. Bullies—Fiction.
4. Colorado—Fiction]   I. Christelow, Eileen, ill.   II. Title.
PZ7.S8250j   1986   [Fic]   86-9941
ISBN 0-02-787880-5

Contents

1.

Let's Study Dinosaurs

Oliver Dibbs came to full attention at Miss Andrews's question. "January is a nice long month, class. What would you like to study?"

One reason Ollie liked his fifth-grade teacher was that she didn't give homework on weekends. Another was that she let them make suggestions about what their class would study.

January was never a very exciting month. There was a letdown after Christmas. And in Boulder they almost never got a snow day, a day when it snowed so much the schools closed. Most of Colorado's big snowstorms came in March and April. January was long and cold. Vacation time was months away.

Ollie was hardly ever bored. But if he was, it was in January. Could he make a suggestion that would make school more exciting?

"Let's study bears," said Rebecca Sawyer before Ollie could think of anything. Rebecca had a huge collection of stuffed bears. "Bears are fascinating animals."

"We studied animals that are endangered," Peter Allman reminded Rebecca and the class. "Bears wouldn't be that different. Let's study airplanes. The history of flying."

Ollie was more interested in animals than he was in airplanes, but they might visit the airport on a field trip. That would be interesting. Peter's father was an airline pilot. He might show them inside a plane.

"Let's study space," Lester Philpott suggested. "Men in space." Lester leaned back in his desk and put his long legs in the aisle. Ollie noticed that Lester's tennis-shoe laces had been broken and tied back together several times.

"Women are in space, too," Rebecca added quickly.

"Lester knows about space," whispered Frank Ashburn, Ollie's best friend. "All that space between his ears."

Lester heard Frank, of course. Frank meant for him to. So did everyone around Frank, and they laughed. Lester gave Frank a look that said, *I'll get you later.*

Ollie smiled at Frank's joke. Lester was a tall, lanky kid who usually made Ollie's life miserable. Ollie would like to send Lester into space for about twenty-five years. But for once he agreed with Lester. A space unit would be neat.

"Sixth grade always has a big space unit," said Miss Andrews. "Remember they sent six students to visit NASA in Dallas this year? Good idea, Lester, but you'll have to wait until next year."

All the fifth-graders were quiet for a minute. Everyone was thinking. Then Ollie remembered the book he'd read and reread while he was tending his recycling stand in the fall. It was about the theory of dinosaurs being warm-blooded. He spoke up quickly.

"How about dinosaurs, Miss Andrews? Some scientists think they were warm-blooded. There's been a lot of new research about what might have killed them off. And we can do some research of our own."

"Hey, good idea, Ollie." Frank seconded Ollie's suggestion. "I'd like to study dinosaurs."

A cheer went up. The pretty teacher smiled but hushed them again. "Mr. Hawkins will be down here to check on us if you get any noisier. All in favor raise your hands." It looked as if everyone but Lester had raised his hand. "Okay, class, dinosaurs it is."

At recess lots of kids came up to Ollie and thanked him for his idea. Ollie felt pleased until he saw Lester kicking a juice carton. For a long time Ollie had thought that Lester hated him. Then one day Rebecca said she thought Lester was jealous of Ollie's good ideas. Although it was hard for Ollie to believe that Lester was jealous of him, Rebecca was good at knowing how people felt. So Ollie had begun to believe her.

Ollie did something he wouldn't usually do, because he avoided Lester when at all possible. He left the crowd of kids around him and walked over to Lester. "You had a good idea, Lester. Too bad we have to wait until next year to blast off into space."

Lester couldn't handle Ollie's being nice to him. "Maybe you can be an astronaut, Dibbs. Help settle

Jupiter and the farthest planets. They'll need people with good ideas. You'll be gone for at least fifty years, and we won't have the pleasure of your company here."

Peter joined them and tried to start a serious conversation. "Think we'll keep on exploring space? They're talking about sending robots or animals up instead of people."

"Pigs—in—Space," Ronnie Swarts said dramatically, thinking of the popular Muppets episode. Ronnie was the smallest boy in class and enjoyed showing off. He swooshed his arms in a flying motion.

"Dibbs—in—Space," Lester echoed, drawing out the words, making Dibbs sound a lot like pigs. He got the laugh he wanted from the crowd of fifth-graders.

Ollie gave up being nice to Lester and walked away. Why had he even tried?

"Don't pay any attention to Lester," Rebecca said to Ollie. "He's jealous because Miss Andrews and the class chose your idea instead of his."

"That's the last time I'll try to be nice to him." Ollie fell into step beside Rebecca. He had stopped being embarrassed at being seen with Rebecca ever since her idea for Halloween had helped him win a prize. She'd worked hard on his successful gray-whale and prairie-dog projects, too. Sometimes he even sought out Rebecca's company. In fact, she and Ollie and Frank had become a threesome. They'd had so much fun over Christmas vacation that they had hated to see school start again. Now maybe January wouldn't be so bad.

After school Ollie told Alice, his sister who was in

4

ninth grade, that he was going to the library. Alice got paid to baby-sit Ollie and his younger brother, Bo. Bo was seven. Ollie's parents both worked and never got home before five-thirty. Ollie figured Alice had the world's easiest job—a *sinecure,* his new word for the day. His mother had given him a new-word calendar for Christmas. All Alice ever did was listen to records or talk on the phone. Ollie took care of Bo.

"You have to take Bo with you, Ollie," Alice said. "And get home before dark." Alice had polished each nail on her left hand navy blue. Now she was drawing squiggles on the blue with a special nail-polish pen.

"Yeah, Ollie. I want to go." Bo liked to tag along after Ollie. He said life with Ollie was always exciting.

"I don't want to have to pay two bus fares," Ollie protested.

"The bus is free, Ollie." Alice grinned. She'd taken care of the only excuse Ollie could think up quickly. He'd forgotten that the city had this experiment of letting people ride the bus free so they'd get in the bus habit.

Ollie sighed and told Bo to get his hat and coat. It was cold and windy. Dolby, the Dibbses' Great Dane and Labrador mix dog, saw people getting ready to go somewhere. He thumped his tail on the hall floor.

"No, Dolby," Ollie said. "You can't go. Dogs aren't allowed in the library."

Taking Bo's hand, Ollie walked the block and a half to the bus stop on Nineteenth Street. The number four bus would stop a block from the Boulder Public Library.

Ollie had timed it so they hopped right on, *clang, clang, clang,* up the cold metal steps.

"There's the prairie-dog boy," a little kid said as he pointed to Ollie. He climbed into his mother's lap, stuck his thumb in his mouth, and stared at Ollie.

Ollie waved to him and looked out the bus window at leaves and trash scudding by. It felt pretty good to know that some people, even little kids, remembered his campaign to save the prairie dogs at C-Mart last fall.

"Boy, you're famous," Bo whispered, smiling at Ollie and sticking his hands in his parka pockets. Bo's brown eyes were enormous. His hat was almost too big and came to his eyebrows, but he'd hardly taken it off since Christmas. Mrs. Dibbs had knitted the stocking hat for Bo. It was red, white, and blue stripes and had a long tail covered with white felt stars. The tail wrapped around Bo's neck like a muffler. "I'm proud to be your brother," Bo added, and smiled again.

Good grief. Why did Bo always have to say that? It made Ollie feel guilty for wishing Bo wouldn't hang around him all the time.

At the library Ollie found he could check out only two books on dinosaurs at a time. He'd read all the ones in the children's library, so he'd selected four in the adult room.

The librarian looked sympathetic when she saw that Ollie was disappointed. "Does your brother have a card? You can check out two on his," she suggested.

Ollie brightened. He read fast, and he wanted enough

books for the rest of the week and the weekend. "Give the lady your library card, Bo." Ollie poked Bo, who was watching a line of preschoolers march by.

"I want to check out some books for myself." Bo handed over the small white card reluctantly.

"There's no limit to how many," the lady said, running a light across the number of each book so that it went into the computer. "It's only per subject." She handed Bo his card along with two of Ollie's books. They headed across the covered bridge to the children's room.

"These are too heavy for me to carry, Ollie." Bo handed Ollie the two books and ran to look out the big windows on the bridge. Way below, Boulder Creek hurried between the two library buildings. It was neat to look right down on it from the picture windows. Ice crusted both edges and, in the shadows of the big trees on either side of the creek, a bit of snow was left from the big storm at Christmas.

In the children's library Bo selected way too many picture books and easy reads, but Ollie couldn't talk him into leaving any behind.

"January is a good time to stay inside and read," said Bo. "Alvin and Gary are both sick, so I have no one to play with. I helped you get all yours, Ollie."

Ollie had no argument for that. "You'll have to carry them yourself. All the way home," he warned. The four adult books that Ollie carried were already getting heavy.

"I can." Bo stacked up the books and smiled at the

man who checked them out for him. They went out the back door of the children's library.

They followed the creek east to get to Broadway and the bus stop. Crossing a wooden bridge with wrought-iron banisters on either side, Ollie set a fast pace. He hoped Bo would keep up. He didn't figure Alice would worry about them, but the days were short and by four o'clock the light was going fast. It was also getting colder with the sun down behind the mountains that lined up all along the western edge of town. Twice Ollie turned around to watch Bo restack his books.

"We should have brought a sack," Bo said. Ollie said nothing. It was too late now to remind Bo he had too many books.

Sitting on a bench on Broadway, the main street of Boulder, they watched a steady stream of cars whiz by. Finally, a number four bus came. Bo tried to get on before the crowd of waiting passengers.

The first step was steep, and Bo managed it, but before he could climb the next two his books slowly slid forward from his arms onto the bus floor. At least they didn't fall into the street.

The driver took one look at the mess and stared out the window, tapping his fingers on the steering wheel. People behind Ollie coughed and cleared their throats, but said nothing. Ollie couldn't get past Bo to help him. The books had plastic covers to protect them, but it made them slide farther. Two had even shot under the driver's seat.

Finally the boys got seated.

"I guess the driver's mad at me," Bo said quietly. He hunched on the inside seat by the window. The library books he had gathered up were stacked high on his lap.

"Probably," Ollie answered, biting his tongue to keep from saying anything else.

They got off the bus at Kalmia with no mishap, but a block from home more trouble appeared. Lester sped by on his bike. He made a sliding stop inches away from Bo's feet. Gravel from the shoulder of the road rattled and thumped Bo's and Ollie's feet and legs. Bo dropped his books again.

"Dibbs—in—Space," Lester hollered as he grabbed Bo's hat and wheeled away, laughing. "At least you'll have something to read while you're out there traveling for fifty years." He held Bo's hat out behind him like a flag.

Ollie knew Lester wouldn't be able to read in space any better than he could on earth, but that didn't make Ollie feel any better. At first Bo ran after Lester. Lester would let him almost catch up, dangling the hat just out of Bo's reach. Then he'd speed away. At the corner of Oakwood, Lester tossed the stocking cap into Mrs. Mitchell's peach tree. The tail hung just out of reach.

"Now what will we do?" asked Bo.

Climbing the small peach tree was no problem for either boy. But both knew Mrs. Mitchell hated kids, boys in particular.

"Maybe she isn't home," Ollie said, hoping. She always put her car in the garage so there was no way of telling.

"I can go ask if we can get it," suggested Bo, "but let's hurry. I'm freezing." Bo's ears were red from the cold and his hands were the same. Ollie hoped he hadn't left his gloves at the library.

"She'll say no. I'll scramble up there and be down before she can look out her window." Ollie set down his books and ran into Mrs. Mitchell's yard. Quickly he shinnied up the tree. He had to reach way out for the hat since the tree limbs were small.

Sure enough, while Ollie was stretched full out, just touching the knit cap, the front door opened and Mrs. Mitchell's sharp voice rang out through the cold air. It was as if she had been watching and waiting for Ollie to climb the tree.

"What are you doing in my peach tree, Oliver Dibbs?"

"Here, Bo, run!" Ollie tossed the cap to Bo and slid, almost falling from the tree. As he hit the ground, Raggs, Mrs. Mitchell's apricot poodle, shot out into the yard, yapping.

"Raggs, come back!" Mrs. Mitchell screamed. Raggs was her baby and was never allowed out alone.

Alice had let Dolby outside, and he heard the commotion from where he stood, waiting for the boys, in the Dibbses' yard. Turning into a black avenger, he streaked after Raggs just as the poodle started nipping at Ollie's heels.

"Dolby, no!" shouted Ollie.

"My baby!" Mrs. Mitchell screamed, moving toward the dogs and Ollie.

Ollie grabbed Dolby's collar and pulled him off his feisty opponent. Dolby wouldn't really hurt Raggs, but he hated the poodle. The two dogs made enough noise for six dogfights.

Tugging Dolby to the street, Ollie grabbed up his books and pulled Dolby until he decided running with Ollie was more fun than fighting with Raggs. He and Bo raced Ollie home, with Mrs. Mitchell still shouting after them.

"Oliver Dibbs, I'm calling your mother. Just see if I don't."

Home safely, Bo looked at Ollie. "Why do you let Lester Philpott pick on you and me all the time, Ollie?" Bo's voice was shaky.

"I don't *let* Lester pick on us," Ollie said, sharper than he meant. He was frustrated with Bo, but mad at Lester. Mrs. Mitchell would call Mrs. Dibbs, and Ollie would end up taking the blame for the whole thing.

Lester had always been a problem for Ollie, but he was getting worse. He had tried ignoring Lester, but it wasn't working very well. Sooner or later he knew he was going to have to do something, something that would put Lester in his place for a long time.

2.

Stegosaurus for State Fossil

Just inside the back door, Bo let the books slide onto the family-room couch. "I guess I got too many books, didn't I, Ollie?"

"I guess so." Ollie replied, going into his room so he could read until dinner.

Mrs. Dibbs was warming lasagna and fresh-smelling French bread in the microwave. She'd spread the loaf with butter and garlic. Neither boy had to be called twice to dinner. Ollie put Lester out of his mind. He smiled at Bo to tell him he wasn't really mad at him. And so far Mrs. Mitchell hadn't called. With any luck she'd forget about it this time.

After they ate, he helped his father with the dishes, then curled in a chair with the best of the new dinosaur books. Mr. Dibbs had built a fire in the fireplace and was helping Bo read one of his harder picture books. Everyone was stuffed and warm. Wind howled around the red brick house and occasionally made flames flare up, but the family was cozy. Even Alice was home, working a crossword puzzle in her January copy of *Today's Teens*.

"What's the state bird of Colorado?" she asked. "It's two words and eleven letters." Her pencil poised between two blue-speckled fingernails.

Mrs. Dibbs looked up from her jigsaw puzzle, all fifteen hundred pieces. Ollie had gotten it for her for Christmas. He figured it would take her all of January to work it. "I don't know," she said. "That's awful, isn't it?"

"I confess I don't know, either." Mr. Dibbs shifted Bo to the other side of his lap.

"Lark bunting," answered Ollie. He had learned that in third grade. He figured Alice had, too, but it wasn't something she'd remember.

But feeling proud that he'd known something that Alice didn't left his mind immediately. Her question and something he'd just read triggered a great idea.

Some high-school students in Canyon City, Colorado, had discovered and dug up the Stegosaurus that lives in the Denver Museum of Natural History. If kids could find all those dinosaur bones and dig them up, then Ollie . . .

Wow! This was far and away the best idea that Ollie had ever had. If he pulled it off, he wouldn't just be famous in Boulder. He'd be famous all over the state of Colorado.

The next morning Ollie hurried to school. He was bursting to make his suggestion to the teacher and the class. He knew everyone would be as excited as he was.

He waited through reading class. They had individualized work, meaning you could read anything you wanted, just so long as you were reading. Miss Andrews worked with Lester and a few more kids who were behind grade level. Occasionally she stopped at someone's desk and listened to a student read aloud or discuss his or her book. On Friday anyone who wanted to could give an oral book report. Ollie noticed that today lots of kids were reading dinosaur books.

He waited through math class. They were doing long division. On Fridays they did math games, held contests, or worked at the board. Ollie liked math better when the numbers he worked with were money. His money. He spent a lot of time figuring out how to earn money for all his projects. Right now, Christmas had left him broke. He needed a moneymaking idea badly.

After lunch they had unit studies. Finally. But still Ollie waited for the right moment. Miss Andrews had talked to them about their study of dinosaurs. She wanted each person to write his or her own dinosaur book. It could be about one dinosaur or a general book about all of them. "I also want us to work on one project as a class. Let's brainstorm the kinds of projects we might do."

"We could write a play about dinosaurs," Rebecca

suggested. She was big on plays, Ollie knew. "We could do it for the lower grades."

"We could write a dinosaur magazine," Peter said. He wanted to be a writer.

"We could paint a big mural and hang it in the hall," Frank suggested. "Or do a diorama like at the Denver Museum of Natural History."

"Can we visit the museum?" Rebecca asked. "I always like to go there."

"These are all great ideas." Miss Andrews smiled. She wrote the list on the chalkboard. "And we can probably divide into groups and do several of them. Are there any more ideas?"

Now was his chance. Ollie raised his hand.

"Yes, Ollie?" Miss Andrews had a big smile for him. "You always have good ideas."

"Stegosaurus was discovered in Colorado in 1877. In Golden, not too far from Boulder. A group of high-school students discovered and dug up the Stegosaurus that's in the Denver Museum of Natural History. All states have a state bird and a state flower. A few have a state fossil. I think we should get Stegosaurus elected as state fossil."

No one in the class said anything. No one seemed excited about Ollie's idea. Rebecca, Frank, Peter—all Ollie's friends stared at him as if he'd suggested running for governor himself.

"How could we do that?" Miss Andrews asked when it was obvious no one else was going to say anything.

"I . . . I think we'd have to take the idea to the state senate or the state legislature. They'd have to vote on it to make it a law." Ollie tried to make it sound exciting, but he wasn't sure how they'd go about getting Stegosaurus elected. He hadn't had time to look into the idea that thoroughly.

"Bo—ring," Lester said, with a big yawn.

"Kids can't make up laws," Nolan Schultz said.

"Why not?" Miss Andrews asked. "Who makes up our laws?"

There were several guesses. "The governor?" "The senators?" "The president?"

"Laws *should* come from the people," Miss Andrews continued. "Laws are for the people. I'm afraid I don't know much about the process, either. Does anyone?" Miss Andrews never minded admitting she didn't know things. Ollie knew some adults who pretended they knew everything. They got mad if you suggested they didn't.

No one in the class knew anything about making up laws. Peter had one idea. "Janie Ferrigan from fourth grade is my neighbor. Her mother is in the state senate. Maybe Mrs. Ferrigan would come and talk to us."

"Good idea, Peter, but let's do some research first to see what we can find out about laws. Will anyone volunteer to help Ollie? We won't vote on Ollie's idea until we find out if we can do it."

"I'd rather paint a mural," said Frank, with an apologetic look at Ollie.

"I will," volunteered Peter.

"I guess I will, too." Rebecca wasn't sure, but she sounded willing to try.

Everyone went to recess buzzing with ideas for their study of dinosaurs. Not many were talking about Ollie's great idea, but he wasn't ready to give it up.

"How about Dibbs for state fossil?" Lester shouted before he ran to play kickball.

This time Ollie did ignore him.

3.

Teacher's Pet

Miss Andrews was on duty as recess teacher. Ollie spent the recess time talking to her, and he felt a little better. While she wasn't sold on his idea, she was interested in what he had to say.

When the bell rang signaling them to line up, Lester kicked the ball whizzing past Ollie. Then he scrambled to pick it up and get in line. "Oliver Dibbs, good day, Your Nibs." He bowed to Ollie. "You can bet, he's teacher's pet."

Several people laughed, and three girls in line behind Ollie covered their mouths and giggled.

Miss Andrews stood at the front of the line. "Settle down, class, before we go inside." When it got fairly quiet, she opened the outside door to their classroom and led the way in. Most everyone went to hang up coats, get a drink, or go to the bathroom.

"Ollie," Miss Andrews said quietly to Ollie. He had taken his seat in the front of the class next to the windows. He stared out the window, ignoring everyone. Miss Andrews came to stand by his desk. "I heard what Lester said, Ollie. I like to think we're friends, but if it's giving you problems, we can pretend we're not."

"That's all right, Miss Andrews." Ollie looked at her. She had long blonde hair, friendly brown eyes, and a big smile. Ollie thought she was the prettiest teacher he had ever had. He wanted to think she was his friend. "Lester doesn't bother me. I just ignore what he says."

"That's all you can do, Ollie. Unless you want to try to be his friend. He needs a friend. Since you are my friend, Ollie, I want you to be the first in the class to hear my news. I'm getting married on Valentine's Day. It's no longer a secret, so you can tell anyone you like. I plan to tell the whole class soon since I'll be gone for a week on my honeymoon."

Ollie was speechless. He watched Miss Andrews turn and walk toward the hall to quiet people down again. Getting married? Miss Andrews was getting married? How could she do that? A big lump formed in Ollie's stomach and sat there the rest of the afternoon. He realized it was special for Miss Andrews to share her secret with him before she told the class. She was trying to make him feel better after Lester had teased him. But this news didn't make Ollie feel a bit better.

Rebecca waited for Ollie after school. "When do you

want to find out about laws, Ollie? Peter says if we'll come over, he'll introduce us to his neighbor, Mrs. Ferrigan."

Ollie said nothing. He kept walking beside Rebecca as if she had said nothing, too.

"What's the matter, Ollie? Didn't you hear what I said?"

Ollie burst out with his news. "Miss Andrews is getting married. On Valentine's Day."

Rebecca squealed. "Oh, how wonderful, Ollie! Don't you think that's wonderful? It's so romantic. On Valentine's Day." She bounced up and down a couple of times.

Silly girl. Ollie kicked a rock off the sidewalk.

"Ollie!" Rebecca laughed. "You're jealous. That's what's wrong with you. I tried to get your attention all afternoon after I saw Miss Andrews talking to you. But I could see you were bothered by something. I thought it was Lester's saying you were teacher's pet."

"Aw, I'm not, either. That's the silliest thing I've ever heard. And if you say that to anyone, *anyone,* I'll never tell you any of my good ideas again."

Rebecca grinned and Ollie looked away quickly. "I think it's sweet, Ollie. I love Miss Andrews, too."

Sweet. Ollie wanted to throw up. All of a sudden Rebecca was acting just like a girl. Why had Ollie ever thought he wanted to be friends with a girl?

"None of my teachers ever got married." Rebecca kept talking, not knowing or caring what Ollie thought.

"They were already married or way too old. I'm going to get her a present. Maybe we can go in together on a nice present, Ollie. Want to?"

"Maybe. We'll talk about it later." A whole lot later, Ollie thought. He kept going after Rebecca turned off at her house. She wanted him to stop for a few minutes, but he'd had enough of her silly ideas.

Frank passed Ollie on his bike. Ollie called to him. "Want to play Scrabble, Frank?"

"Can't. I have a dentist appointment." Frank whizzed home.

When Ollie got home, Bo had gone off to Gary Gravenstein's house to play, and Alice was on the phone. It was a January thaw day, mild and sunny. Ollie couldn't find anything he wanted to eat, so he just sat on the front step with his arm around Dolby. Dolby was glad for the attention, and although he had trouble sitting still, he looked at Ollie often and licked his face once. Ollie was glad someone understood. His new word for the day was *ebullient*. It meant joyful or excited. He sure didn't feel ebullient.

Ollie got through dinner without anyone's asking why he was so quiet. But at bedtime his father came up to Bo and Ollie's room. "What's the matter, Ollie? You hardly touched the eggplant parmigiana. You used to love it."

"Oh, nothing." Ollie felt silly sharing what was really wrong, even though Bo was asleep and only Dad would hear him.

His dad sat on the edge of the bed. "Talking about it might help."

After a minute Ollie asked, "Did you ever like any of your teachers a lot? A whole lot?"

Dad didn't laugh. Ollie was grateful. His dad sat thinking for a minute. "I haven't thought about Miss Vickers for a long time, Ollie. She was my fourth-grade teacher, and I was in love with her. I had big plans to marry her when I grew up."

"Marry her?" Even Ollie knew that was dumb.

"Yep. She got married in June after school was out, and it took me two years to forgive her. She didn't stop teaching, but I could never call her Mrs. Utterback."

"Mrs. Utterback?" Now Ollie smiled.

"Awful name to trade for, wasn't it? Women didn't keep their own names then or hyphenate them the way they do now."

Ollie felt a little better. "Mrs. Utterback," he said again, and managed to laugh.

"Yeah," Dad said again, and laughed quietly, too. "Good-night, Ollie," he whispered so as not to wake up Bo. He leaned over and kissed Ollie, something he didn't do often anymore.

"Good-night, Dad," Ollie answered. "And thanks." He lay there for a long time. "Mrs. Utterback," he whispered. Finally he fell asleep.

4.

Bo's Birthday Spoiled

Ollie got down to breakfast the next morning before Bo, who was always slow getting up and dressed. His father's suitcase sat in the hall at the bottom of the stairs.

"Ollie," Mom said, as she turned the good-smelling bacon and sipped her coffee. "Your father has to go out of town unexpectedly. You know I promised Bo a birthday party on Saturday, which happens to be tomorrow, and I don't feel like tackling it alone. Alice promised to help on a school project, and it *is* her day off."

Since Alice baby-sat all week, Mrs. Dibbs tried to give her weekends for her friends and activities.

"I'm sorry this is so last minute," Dad said. "I tried to get out of going, and I hate to miss the party. If I give you five dollars, Ollie, will you help out? Do the entertainment?" Mr. Dibbs was eating quickly while he glanced at the newspaper.

"I'll give you some money for a few more party favors, too," Mrs. Dibbs said, "before you leave for school. I won't have time to shop again."

Ollie felt bombarded by people asking him to do things. And entertaining a bunch of seven-year-old boys would be hard work. It might be worth more than five dollars. But since Bo was his brother, Ollie figured he should help out even without pay. But it would take a good plan. And it *was* tomorrow. Ollie looked at Alice, who made a face at him. You might know she'd get out of helping.

"I'll try to think of something," Ollie promised, quickly hiding the money his dad handed him. Bo came in looking sleepy. He was wearing a T-shirt that made him look like a bumblebee.

"Look at this headline, Ollie." Mr. Dibbs winked and changed the subject. He folded his newspaper over and handed the section to Ollie. "Maybe you should get a license to hunt dinosaurs instead of studying them."

Ollie read part of the article aloud. Even Dolby listened and thumped his tail. " 'As advertisement to make people want to vacation in Utah, the chamber of commerce in Vernal, Utah, gives out dinosaur licenses.' "

"They sound desperate." Alice twisted a strand of hair over her finger as she waited for the eggs. "But then, who'd want to vacation in Utah?"

"Utah is beautiful." Mom placed a big platter of bacon and scrambled eggs on the table. Ollie remembered he hadn't eaten any dinner.

"I want one," said Bo, coming awake at the idea. "Are they free?"

"Yeah, I want one, too." Ollie took out his ball-point pen. "I'll order us both one."

Before he left for school, Ollie addressed an envelope: Al E. Oup, Deputy Lizard Warden, Vernal, Utah 84078. Inside he included a piece of notebook paper that read, *Please send me twenty-six dinosaur licenses.* The article had said that some people ordered lots to give as jokes. Ollie didn't know what he'd do with twenty-four licenses, but it seemed like a good idea to order more than two, as long as it was okay.

At the end of the letter, he added that his class was studying dinosaurs. That way they might think he was writing for the class, too, in case they hesitated to send a kid so many licenses. He put the letter in their mailbox as he and Bo left to walk to school. Their carrier would pick it up when he delivered the mail.

Ollie knew he needed to do some good thinking about Bo's birthday party. He used the walking time to think, but nothing came to him. As soon as he got in his seat at school, he pulled out his dinosaur book and started to read. He tried not to worry. He didn't always know where his good ideas came from, but often they just popped into his head.

Sure enough, during reading class the words *hunt* and *dinosaur* came together and *wham*. Ollie knew what to plan to entertain Bo's guests. He'd set up a dinosaur hunt! He'd hide clues early in the morning. Each would lead to the next until the final clue led to a big dinosaur.

Whoever found it first would get a nice prize. He didn't know if he'd hide plastic dinosaurs or pictures, but he'd figure that out tonight. He'd write the clues first.

All day long he worked on the clues. No one questioned what he was doing since he had three dinosaur books open around him. Miss Andrews had announced that the afternoon would be devoted to independent study and research for their books.

Ollie's first clue read like this:

> Leave the yard, start down the street.
> This dinosaur loved others to eat.
> ALLOSAURUS

He'd put Allosaurus by the Johnsons' hedge. The next clue read:

> Tyrannosaurus was the king.
> Find a bell that you can't ring.
> TYRANNOSAURUS REX

Ollie traced the neighborhood in his mind. There was a Mountain Bell sign on the corner of Oakwood, saying a telephone cable was buried there. He'd hide the Tyrannosaurus there.

On and on he wrote, finding his rhymes the most fun he'd had all week. He forgot other things he was worried about.

> This dinosaur had a sail.
> The next clue is under a whale.
> SPINOSAURUS

27

Ollie would hide that clue under the big papier-mâché whale he still had in the garage.

> This dinosaur had plates and spikes.
> Find a clue close to the bikes.
> ANKLYOSAUR

He hoped Bo's friends could read well enough to follow the clues. He'd have to stay outside to help them. Maybe his mother would help, too. She hadn't asked him to run the party, just help with some entertainment.

Ollie made ten clues in all. The last three read:

> This dinosaur had horns and bony frills
> To protect his head from enemies and chills.
> TRICERATOPS

Not the best rhythm, but he wanted to hide the clue in the Dibbses' refrigerator.

> One of the biggest ate mostly plants.
> His brain was only the size of an ant's.
> BRONTOSAURUS

Bo would remember how they'd fought the ants that swarmed around the two new aspen trees in their yard. Ollie would hang Brontosaurus on a low limb of one of the trees. The book said that Brontosaurus's brain was as big as a pea, but he needed a word that would rhyme with "plant." The closest he could come was "plant . . . ant." The idea was the same. Dinosaurs had very small brains. Most plant-eating dinosaurs were

pretty dumb for their size. They operated by feelings instead of brain power. Brontosaurus lead to the winner, which Ollie would hide under Bo's big sailboat model in his room.

> This dinosaur needs your vote.
> He's hidden by a big sailboat.
> STEGOSAURUS

He'd tell the boys about Stegosaurus for state fossil, an idea he hadn't forgotten. He'd just postponed it until after this birthday party.

Ollie wished he could give all of Bo's guests dinosaur hunting licenses, but they wouldn't come in time.

He finished the game just as school was out. He could hardly wait to get home. He needed to go over to C-Mart and look for a good prize. Also, he hadn't gotten Bo a present yet himself. He had saved up two dollars and fifty cents from his allowance since Christmas, but he was waiting for some miracle to get more. Sometimes money came to him when he needed it, just like ideas, but he figured he'd earn the five dollars his dad had given him that morning.

People shouldn't have birthdays so close to Christmas. But Bo couldn't help when he was born. And January was almost over. Tomorrow was the twenty-fourth.

Alice had told Bo he could go to Gary's again. Mrs. Gravenstein should get half of Alice's baby-sitting money, Ollie thought. But he didn't have time to bug Alice right then.

"I'm going to C-Mart, Alice," he told her.

"What are you getting Bo for his birthday, Ollie?" Alice asked. She was knitting some argyle socks. She said all the girls were making and wearing them, and Alice had to do what everyone else was doing. She didn't like being different like Ollie. Ollie didn't plan to be different. It just worked out that way most of the time.

"I don't know. I'll find something at C-Mart." Ollie left before Alice could decide to go along with him.

"I'm riding my bike, Dolby," Ollie told the big dog, who was sure he could go with Ollie. "Oh, all right." Ollie put his bike back in the garage and got Dolby's leash. "You're right. I might have too much to carry."

Dolby pulled Ollie up the bike path, across the two busy streets that led to C-Mart. Whoever invented the phrase *Walk the dog* didn't have one like Dolby. Dolby walked people.

Ollie had good luck shopping. He found a bag of plastic dinosaurs for the dinosaur-hunt prize. If more than one boy won he could open the package and divide them up. He got balloons, some funny hats, and the candles and candy letters his mom had given him money for. Then he found the perfect gift for Bo. It was a big box of dinosaurs with a plastic swamp to set up around them. It cost him his whole seven dollars, but he liked it, and he knew Bo would, too. Funny how it was turning into a dinosaur birthday. In fact, Ollie's life had become a dinosaur life.

Saturday dawned crispy cold, but clear. Mrs. Dibbs

breathed a sigh of relief. "I can't imagine ten seven-year-olds stuck inside all afternoon."

"Me, either." Ollie mopped his French toast in maple syrup. Bo was still asleep. Alice had left to work on her school project. "Why did you let Bo invite so many kids?"

"I didn't. I said he could ask five. But you know Bo. And who can I un-invite now?" Mrs. Dibbs sighed again and fortified herself with another cup of coffee.

Ollie hid the dinosaur clues, telling his mother to keep Bo inside if he woke up before Ollie got back. Ollie had ended up drawing dinosaurs on tablet cardboards he had saved. It was the best way to get the pictures he wanted, anyway, since he had to have specific dinosaurs to match the clues. He hid the clues in easy places or plain sight, remembering that Bo and his friends were three years younger than he was.

While Ollie was on his way home to hide the ones in the Dibbses' yard, Lester rode past him and hollered in a singsongy voice, "Hey, Oliver Dibbs. How come your mother let you go out and play this early?"

Lester had a paper route and was probably just getting home from his deliveries. He delivered the Dibbses' papers, and Ollie's mom thought he did a good job. Ollie tried to ignore Lester, but Lester circled back to see what Ollie was doing.

"What are you doing? Campaigning for state fossil?" Lester saw the stack of dinosaur pictures. "Fossil: a person whose ideas are out-of-date. Get it?" Lester practically fell off his bike laughing as he quoted the second dictionary definition of a fossil. "You'll get my vote."

"Does your father help you read the dictionary every night, Lester, to lull you to sleep?" Ollie knew he shouldn't tease Lester about his reading ability, but he couldn't hold back his anger any longer.

Lester's face got red. He popped a wheelie, spun around, and took off toward home. But not before he said, "I'll get you, Dibbs, teacher's pet."

Ollie put Lester out of his mind and quickly hid the rest of the dinosaur-hunt clues—except for the one under Bo's boat. He'd wait until Mom took Bo shopping. Mom said she'd take Bo to lunch and bring him back just before the party started. She'd made a list for Ollie:

Put letters on cake. (It's frosted and hidden in
   the microwave.)
Blow up balloons and hang in dining room.
Hang up crepe-paper streamers.
Wrap favors I bought. (They're in the oven.)
Put plastic birthday cloth on the dining table.
Put out Dad's and my gift. (In downstairs
   freezer.)

Mom was good at hiding stuff. Bo had been snooping all week, but he hadn't found a thing.

"Happy birthday, Bo," Ollie said, when he came in and saw Bo eating breakfast.

"Thanks, Ollie. I'm going shopping for some new clothes."

"I know. Where is the list of your friends who are coming to the party?"

Bo stood up, his fork in his fist. "Gary, Brian, Mark," he started to recite the list.

"Wait, wait." Ollie got a pencil to write down the boys' names. "How about Alvin?" Alvin Stenboom and Gary Gravenstein were Bo's two best friends.

"Alvin might be sick." Bo licked the maple syrup that had dribbled down his hand.

"Might be?" Ollie questioned.

"Well, he has been sick. If we're going to play outside, he can come only for cake. He's had a cough too long now."

"You're going to play outside." Mrs. Dibbs pulled on her coat. "Hurry up, Bo. I'll start the car."

Ollie got all the jobs done with no one to bother him, but he wished he'd asked Frank or Rebecca to come over and help. They could have talked about Stegosaurus for state fossil and made some plans. But he hadn't. He made a peanut butter and strawberry jam sandwich for lunch and decided the place looked pretty good. Birthdays were a big deal at the Dibbses', so they had lots of decorations. Bo and Mom would be surprised when they came home.

They were. Bo jumped up and down and clapped. Then he ran to answer the doorbell, and kids started pouring in.

"The traffic was awful, and the shopping center a zoo." Mrs. Dibbs hurried to get her share of the party ready. "Everyone's shopping while the weather's nice."

Ollie helped the boys play some games outside, like tag and red rover. But after two boys cried when Jimbo Wilson "came over" too hard, he decided it was time for the dinosaur hunt. Jimbo weighed about twice as much as Bo, making the rest of the first-graders look like dwarfs. He'd been held back in first grade for another year.

Ollie explained the game twice and then gave the boys the first clue. They took off toward the corner when Ollie hinted the first dinosaur was hidden in that direction. Oakwood was a dead-end street, which was nice because it had less traffic.

He watched them pass the Allosaurus clue that he had leaned in plain sight against the Johnsons' hedge. No one could miss it. They ran all the way to the corner where Tyrannosaurus was hidden. Soon they came back, led by Bo.

"This is too hard, Ollie," Bo complained. "You hid them in too hard places."

"They're in plain sight, Bo." Ollie started down the street and all the boys followed him, practically knocking him over when he stopped to look. Allosaurus was gone. He ran to the corner. Tyrannosaurus wasn't by the Mountain Bell sign.

Then he ran back home and into the garage. No clue under the whale. None by the bikes. He looked in the other places. The one in the fridge was there, and he guessed the one under Bo's boat was in place. But all the other clues that Ollie had hidden were gone.

5.

Dolby and the Brontosaurus

It didn't take Ollie long to figure out what had happened. Lester. He was the only one who'd seen Ollie hiding clues. While Ollie was inside, decorating or eating lunch, Lester had followed up the clues and taken them, along with the pictures.

"Mom," Ollie said. His mother had come out to see what all the commotion was about. "I think someone took all the clues I put out for the dinosaur game."

"Who would do such a thing, Ollie? And why?" Mrs. Dibbs was puzzled.

"Lester did it, didn't he, Ollie? He hollered at me when we came home from shopping. He said, 'Happy birthday, Bo.' How did he know it was my birthday? Why did you let Lester spoil my birthday, Ollie?" Bo began to cry.

"I didn't *let* him ruin the game, Bo. We don't know he did it." Ollie turned to his mother. He couldn't handle Bo's crying, or the party's being spoiled.

"Think fast, Ollie," Mrs. Dibbs pleaded. She didn't know what to do with a houseful of seven-year-old boys, either.

Ollie looked at his watch. He was still thinking dinosaurs. "How would you feel about driving us to the Denver Museum of Natural History, Mom? We could see the real dinosaurs there."

"Yeah!" Bo stopped crying immediately. "Good idea, Ollie."

"I guess I could live through that," Mom said slowly. It seemed she wasn't sure. "You'll all have to be quiet in the car."

"We will," chorused all the seven-year-old voices.

"I guess I should call everyone's mother," Mrs. Dibbs said as an afterthought.

"There's no time, Mom," Ollie said. "They won't care." They probably wouldn't care if Mom kept their kids for a week, Ollie thought.

Mrs. Dibbs handed out Black Cow suckers and the favors she'd bought earlier, which were those BB games where you make the BBs roll into little holes for a score. Maybe the games would entertain the boys in the car. And with a Black Cow in their mouths they couldn't talk much.

"Come on, Bo," Ollie called, as everyone else headed for the car.

"Wait," said Bo. "I have to make a phone call first."

Bo had hung up the phone when Ollie came back for him. "I have to go to the bathroom," he announced.

"Okay, okay." Ollie hoped no one heard him and

got the same idea. They'd never get to the museum before it closed.

All the boys and Dolby piled into the station wagon. Ollie tried to count to make sure everyone was there but quickly gave up. Mrs. Dibbs said it would be cool enough for Dolby to stay in the car while they went inside the museum. Dogs weren't allowed to tour, of course. Too many old bones, Ollie thought, and smiled.

He sat up front with his mother and Jimbo Wilson, who told them about his mother and father's divorce. True to their word, the boys were fairly quiet until Dolby took Sam Satori's Black Cow sucker.

"Look, he can't open his mouth," Sam said, instead of being unhappy about the loss.

Ollie turned around to see Dolby pawing at his teeth, trying to get his jaws apart.

"Good grief," said Mrs. Dibbs, her eyes on the traffic while Dolby finally swallowed his newly acquired treat.

The Denver Museum of Natural History had a big grizzly bear out front. First the boys ran to see it, then they lined up while Mrs. Dibbs bought tickets. As they went through the turnstile, Ollie said, "Take hands. Everyone get a partner."

At first everyone wanted to walk with Bo, but he finally took Alvin's hand on one side and Gary's on the other. Ollie took Jimbo Wilson's since he got left out.

"Wow, look at that," Bo said, and the boys spread out around the giant skeleton of Brontosaurus.

Ollie was impressed, too. He always was, no matter how many times he came here and saw the real size of a dinosaur. It was one thing to read about a creature eighty feet long, another to see it. "Did you know that the biggest dinosaur here, Brachiosaurus, weighed eighty-five tons? That is one hundred and seventy *thousand* pounds," Ollie told Jimbo.

"No kidding." Jimbo's mouth hung open as he looked at the huge skeleton. "He's bigger than I am, isn't he?"

"He sure is." Ollie knew Jimbo took a lot of teasing about being the biggest first-grader in the school.

They went to see Stegosaurus, and Ollie imagined a plaque in front of it next year. The plaque would read NEWLY ELECTED STATE FOSSIL. CAMPAIGN LED BY OLIVER DIBBS. He smiled and stood up a little straighter.

The hour that was left before the museum closed went fast. Everyone was hungry, so the boys piled into the car, eager to get home. They petted Dolby, who barked and barked. He had been lonely, waiting in the back of the station wagon.

Five o'clock traffic was heavy even on Saturday. Mrs. Dibbs maneuvered onto Colorado Boulevard and headed north to find the turnpike. It had gotten dark while they were inside the museum. The boys in the backseat talked about the dinosaur skeletons. The boys in the very back of the wagon tumbled and wrestled with Dolby. They weren't too loud, so Mrs. Dibbs didn't say anything.

"Look for the sign that says TO BOULDER, Ollie," Mrs. Dibbs said. "I think we can get on the turnpike from here."

Suddenly Bo shouted from the very back of the car.

"Hey, Mom, wait! Stop! Where's Alvin?"

"Alvin?" Mrs. Dibbs pulled off onto a side street as soon as she could find one.

"I thought Alvin couldn't come," Ollie said.

"He couldn't come if we played outside. I told him I'd call when we had refreshments. Instead I called before we left the house. He came right over when he heard we'd be inside the museum." The end of Bo's sentence trailed off.

"Are you sure he was with us?" Mrs. Dibbs asked. She didn't sound like she was in a very good mood, Ollie thought. And now he remembered seeing Alvin holding Bo's hand. It hadn't sunk in until just this minute.

"Yeah," Bo said quietly. "He was in the car before." All the boys were very still.

"Are you sure he's not in the car now?" Mrs. Dibbs asked hopefully.

"Yeah." Several boys echoed Bo's answer.

Mrs. Dibbs gave a very big sigh and put her head down on the steering wheel for a moment. The boys got even quieter. Finally she said, "One day I'm going to wake up and my hair will be a very deep shade of gray. I don't know why it isn't all gray now."

Ollie never saw any of the gray his mother talked about when things went wrong. He thought his mother's hair was a very pretty shade of yellow. He guessed it was just an expression. Turning the car around, she drove back to the museum.

40

"The museum was closing when we left." Ollie hated to remind her.

"Well, they'll just have to open it back up. Alvin must be in there someplace."

"He might be standing out in front right now," Gary said.

"Yeah, in the cold. He'll have the flu again and his mother will kill him," Bo added.

"If I don't first," Mrs. Dibbs muttered. Ollie figured he was the only one who had heard her.

Mrs. Dibbs let Ollie and Jimbo out to check the front of the museum. Some lights were on, but the grizzly bear looked even bigger in the shadows. They didn't see Alvin anywhere.

"Maybe there's a back door," Ollie suggested when they got back in the car, shivering from the cold wind that had come up.

They circled the museum until they saw a few cars parked close-by another lighted door.

"Okay," Mom said, stopping the car. "I want everyone, that's *everyone*, to stay right here in the car. Ollie and I will go see if Alvin's waiting here or if we can get in the museum. Don't get out of the car. Don't speak to anyone. Do you understand?"

"Yes, Mom," the carload of small boys chorused. Dolby thumped his tail on the back floor of the wagon. Bo sat on his knees with his arm around the big dog.

There was a guard in a uniform at the side door of the museum. He wore a gun and had a big flashlight

on his belt. Mrs. Dibbs asked about Alvin.

"No, ma'am. We didn't find a boy when we locked up. You sure you left him in here?"

"Where else could he be?" Mom sounded really worried now.

Then something got their attention. They were standing with the door partly open. Before anyone could think what to do, a big, furry object bolted past them, knocking Ollie aside.

"Dolby! Dolby, come back!" Ollie shouted. "Dogs aren't allowed in the museum."

Ollie took off after the big dog. Mrs. Dibbs took off after Ollie. The guard shouted, "Hey, wait a minute. Come back here." He charged after them. In no time at all, a trail of seven-year-old boys pounded along behind all of them. Jimbo Wilson puffed as he brought up the rear. "Wait, guys. Wait for me."

"Stop, Dolby, stop," Ollie yelled, still running.

Huge shadows quivered on the walls of the museum. Ollie's voice sounded as if he were in a tunnel. His footsteps echoed around him. Dinosaurs loomed out of the darkness, reaching for him.

Ollie stopped looking at the exhibits and hollered again, "Please stop, Dolby!"

When Dolby did stop, Ollie practically fell over him. Dolby's toenails screeched on the tile floor. Then he started dancing back and forth, barking for all he was worth. The Brontosaurus skeleton was the biggest pile of bones he had ever seen. It was scary, too.

"Hush, Dolby, hush." Ollie tried to grab Dolby's collar.

Suddenly Dolby stopped barking. He sat down at what he figured was a safe distance from the monster in front of him. He remembered the sound he'd discovered after hearing a recording of wolf calls back in the fall.

Dolby's howl echoed through the dimly lit rooms that housed the dinosaur skeletons.

6.

Kids Can Make Laws

The sound, bouncing off the rooms empty of people, sent shivers through Ollie. He noticed how shadows closed in around them. The room smelled musty as if from the age of the huge creatures.

Standing in the doorway, the guard flicked his flashlight around the room. Dolby, caught in the beam, immediately stopped howling and squinted his eyes.

"Dolby!" Mrs. Dibbs caught up to them. She scolded the big dog. "Bad boy! Get him out of here, Ollie."

"I'm trying." Ollie took a better hold of Dolby's collar. Dolby didn't want to leave the museum. He had made a wonderful discovery. He started barking again.

Ollie dragged him across the tile floor, Dolby's toenails scraping all the way. Then suddenly Dolby's ears shot to attention and he trotted along willingly. That is, until they reached the next room, which was filled with all sorts of mineral rocks. Pulling Ollie behind him, he ran over to a case and started barking again. Ollie could barely make out something moving in the geology display. Was some ancient fossil coming alive?

"Hi, Ollie." The shadow stood up. "Is it time to go? Why is it so dark in here?"

"Mom," yelled Ollie. "I think we've found Alvin."

Sure enough, the shadow was not a ghost of a long-ago Ichthyosaurus, but Alvin. Mrs. Dibbs was partly relieved, partly angry. "However did you get left behind, Alvin?"

"I . . . I guess I went to sleep. Mom gave me an extra dose of cough syrup before she'd let me come with you guys. It always makes me sleepy." Alvin patted Dolby's head. "Hi, Dolby. What are you doing here?" Dolby's tail thumped the floor of the room. The sound made a hollow *bonk, bonk, bonk* around them.

"Alvin!" Bo hollered. "There you are. Hey, it's scary in here at night." Bo and his friends filled the room, making it much less scary.

"I told you to stay in the car." Mrs. Dibbs backed up to a wall. She looked exhausted. The guard stood beside her. He seemed to have lost his voice.

"Dolby had to go to the bathroom really bad, Mom. So I let him out and then he ran after you guys. I tried to get him to come back but . . . ."

"Never mind," Mrs. Dibbs said. "Can we go home now?"

"Yeah. We have to eat the cake, gang." Bo grinned. "And open presents."

Ollie figured Bo had had a birthday he wouldn't

forget for a while. Mom wouldn't, either. It had turned out to be fun, though. Ollie had always wondered what the museum, with all those skeletons, looked like at night.

Things were quiet for a few days after the party. Bo played with his new games and toys. Mr. Dibbs returned and heard all about the museum trip. Mrs. Dibbs said that from now on work was going to be easy. She ran a computer on her job. Machines were more predictable than people, she told them. She enjoyed machines.

On Sunday Ollie and Peter and Rebecca stopped by to talk to Mrs. Ferrigan about the dinosaur law.

"First you need a sponsor for any bill you introduce to the senate, Ollie. Let me look into it. I think I would be willing to sponsor Stegosaurus for state fossil. You say other states have state fossils?"

"Yes, Mrs. Ferrigan. Eight that we know of. Massachusetts has a dinosaur track, but no state has a dinosaur."

"And you want me to come and talk to your class?"

"Oh, would you, Mrs. Ferrigan?" Rebecca begged. "No one in our class thinks kids can make up a law. We need you to tell them that we can. They'll believe you since you're a state senator."

"Of course kids can make up a law, Rebecca. Especially if it's a good law, an important one."

"I think recognizing Stegosaurus by making it state fossil is important, Mrs. Ferrigan," said Ollie. "It was first found in Colorado by high-school kids. If they could find it, we can put it in a law."

"You have a convincing argument, Ollie." Mrs. Ferrigan smiled at the delegation that had come to her house. "I have a book about Colorado government, too. Would you like to borrow it? It has a section about laws."

"That's just what we need, Mrs. Ferrigan," Peter said. "Thanks."

Ollie and his friends took the book over to Peter's house. His mother gave them cocoa and cookies while they read out loud the part on making laws.

"You three are certainly ambitious," Mr. Allman stopped by to say. He grabbed a cookie. He wasn't flying that day. "When I was your age, all I did was play marbles."

"It was Ollie's idea," Rebecca said. She smiled at Ollie, who looked quickly back to the book.

They copied out a simple explanation about how a bill becomes a law. The next day Miss Andrews let them give a report to the class. On the board Ollie printed some steps. Then he and Peter and Rebecca explained them.

"The proposed law is called a bill," Ollie said first. "Only a member of the state senate or legislature can propose a bill, but the bill can be suggested by anyone. Even a kid."

"Mrs. Ferrigan said she would propose the bill of Stegosaurus for state fossil for us," Peter told them, "after she looks it over, if we agree we want to do this."

"Someone writes the bill," Rebecca continued. "And they check to see if it will cost people any money. Having a state fossil wouldn't cost anyone anything."

Ollie pointed to the steps he had written on the board.

1. Mrs. Ferrigan proposes the bill to the senate since she is a senator.

2. The bill is assigned to a committee.

3. The committee studies it and talks about it.

4. They read it to the senate a second time and debate it. Then they vote on it. If it passes,

5. They read it a third time the next day. They call the roll of members. Each member says yes or no.

6. If it passes the roll call, it goes to the other house—in this case, the legislature, since Mrs. Ferrigan introduces it in the senate. It goes through all the steps again.

7. If the legislature passes it, it goes to the governor for him to sign.

Ollie finished telling the steps by saying, "The shortest time a bill can take to become a law is three days. But it usually takes several weeks. If we decide to do this we have to work to convince people it's a good law. We have to write letters to the senate and maybe the legislature, too. We have to make all the people in Colorado aware of the proposed law. They'll call the state capitol and say they want it passed."

"This sounds like a lot of work," Lester said. His tone of voice said, *Too much work.*

"Lester is right," Miss Andrews said. "If we propose

this law we have to work to get other people interested. We'd need to convince them it's important. But all your life you could say this was *your* law. That you helped get it passed."

"That would be neat," several kids in the class said.

"We *could* make a law."

"Our dinosaur would be elected."

"Stegosaurus for state fossil!" Ollie shouted suddenly, still standing in front of the class like a cheerleader.

"Yea!" the class cheered.

"All in favor?" Miss Andrews asked for a vote.

"Yes," the class shouted again.

"All opposed?" Miss Andrews said. She waited. The class got very quiet. Several people looked at Lester. He took his feet out of the aisle and started poking in his desk.

"The idea passes," Miss Andrews said at last. "Now let's talk about what we'll have to do next."

Ollie felt as if he was going to pop. Everyone was finally excited about his idea. Even Lester hadn't had the nerve to vote against it.

7.

Dinosaur Polaroids

Ollie found that the work had only just begun. Mrs. Ferrigan came to their class, and this time everyone got into the discussion. She got excited, too, and agreed to propose the bill.

"You will have to work to make people aware of it, however. If people write to their senators and legislators and say that they are in favor of a bill, it helps to get it passed. We listen to what the people say."

"We could write to everyone we know," Rebecca suggested.

"I can write an article for the school newspaper, and we could write letters to the editor telling students how to get in touch with their senators and legislators," Peter added.

"Good ideas." Mrs. Ferrigan got ready to leave. "And I think you should send some students to testify at the senate meeting."

"Testify?" Ollie wasn't sure what that meant. He had only heard of a witness testifying in a court trial.

"You need to tell the committee why *you* think the bill is important. Why you think Stegosaurus should be state fossil."

Ollie thought that might be a little scary, but if he had to do it, he would.

"Do you want to be on our committee to testify, Ollie?" Miss Andrews asked.

"I guess so," Ollie answered.

At the dinner table that night Ollie announced, "I'm going to testify at the state senate." He got everyone's attention with the remark. He smiled.

"My goodness," his mother said. "Who are you going to testify against?"

"Lester," Bo said. "Tell how he spoiled our game."

"No, not Lester," Ollie said. "And you don't know he took the stuff. You didn't see him take it." Ollie tried to be fair, and, after all, the birthday party had turned out pretty neat, anyway. "I'm going to testify *for* someone. For Stegosaurus." Ollie told them about what their class was doing and that it was his idea.

"I hope no one asks what my little brother is doing now," Alice said, helping herself to seconds on the candied carrots. "I hope you aren't going to be in the newspaper again, getting a dinosaur elected to something."

"I think that's a wonderful idea, Ollie." Mr. Dibbs's job was studying the Sun. He had helped build a solar observatory; he watched solar flares and eclipses. But he was a person who had many interests. Ollie was glad that these included his projects. Ollie's father smiled. "You can always say that this was your law."

"I think it's my class's law by now." Ollie knew he couldn't do all the work ahead by himself. He'd have to share being famous with his class. But he had thought of the idea. Knowing that the idea was his gave him a big, warm glow inside.

After dinner Ollie went to his room for some serious thinking time. He knew he would need some money for this project. Maybe the school would help with their campaign since it was a school activity. But he might want to do some work on the side, like Xerox flyers and hand them out, or make posters to hang everywhere. And things like that cost money.

Asking people to donate for this particular project just wouldn't be right, he felt. He needed to make a list of ways he could earn money.

Ollie always made lists. He found it helped him think, or it helped him get things done if he had a lot of chores or plans. His mother had taught him to make lists. She said if she didn't have a list, she would probably forget to go to work. Ollie doubted that, but he'd seen the value of writing things down. He had a new journal that his mom had given him for Christmas, and he liked writing in it to help him think.

He thought and thought and came up with a short list of what he could do to earn money.

Baby-sit.

Shovel walks.

Give birthday parties. (entertainment only)

Have a wake-up service.

Walk dogs.

Feed pets and water plants for people on
vacation.

Sell something. (like the garage-sale items at the
recycling stand)

Make and sell something. (like crafts)

As soon as he ran out of ideas for the job list, he ran
back through it to think about each thing.

Baby-sit. He wasn't allowed to baby-sit until he was
twelve. His mom occasionally made an exception, like
when he watched Gary and Alvin and Bo on Saturday
afternoons. But Alvin had been sick, and also it was a
slow, unreliable way to make money. He wanted to
make money fast.

Shovel Walks. There was no snow and none in sight,
so shoveling walks was out for now. Besides, it was
hard work. Surely he could do something easier.

Give Birthday Parties. He thought of Bo's birthday
party and decided to skip that activity unless it was his
only choice.

Have a Wake-up Service. Hmmm. He'd never tried
that but he had read about someone who did it. "Think,
Ollie." His father's words came back to him. "Think
before you act." What could happen? More importantly,
what could go wrong? Ollie made another list.

He'd have an important client, a business man who needed to catch an airplane.

> There would be a big snow.
> Ollie's electricity would go off so that the alarm
>   wouldn't ring.
> He wouldn't wake up.
> The client would miss the plane.
> He'd lose a fortune on a big business deal.
> It would be Ollie's fault.

Maybe Ollie wasn't ready for that kind of responsibility. He went on to the next item on his list.

Walk Dogs. Possible, but it took a lot of time and didn't pay too well. It wasn't quick money, but it was definitely possible.

Shovel Doggy-do from People's Yards. Ollie thought of something that wasn't on his list. But he dismissed it immediately. He did enough of that at home, and it wasn't much fun.

Feed Pets and Water Plants for People on Vacation. Who took a vacation in January? Maybe some skiers, but he didn't think this business would boom right now. Maybe next summer.

Sell Something. He'd closed his most successful business, his recycling stand, for the winter. The good weather they were having now wouldn't last. People usually didn't go looking for garage sales until late spring or summer. And at this time of year, they didn't clean out basements and attics and decide to get rid of stuff, so there wouldn't be any rummage around for

Ollie to recycle. No, he'd better leave his stand closed until summer.

Make and Sell Something. What could he make to sell that anyone could possibly want, especially adults?

He decided to start another list, but suddenly he remembered something—the gift his mom had given his dad for Christmas. If he could borrow it . . . and . . .

He left his list and ran downstairs. Out of the hall closet he took a big pile of photo albums. They went way back. Pictures of him and Bo as a baby. Pictures of Dolby as a puppy. They were funny and fun to look at but he didn't have time now. He pulled out another album. There were pictures of his mother and father getting married. Look how pretty Mom was. But getting married—he didn't want to think about that. He reached for an album whose cover was worn and old-fashioned looking.

Finally, he'd found what he was looking for. Pictures of his grandmother when she was young. He laughed. In one Gramma sat on a big crescent moon. She leaned on the curve of the moon and smiled. In another only her face showed. That was the one that Ollie had re-membered. Gramma stood behind a cardboard cutout of a woman in a funny bathing suit. The cutout had no head. When Gramma stood behind it, you could think she was the woman in the funny suit.

Clickity-clickity-click. The wheels in Ollie's brain spun around. It was a great idea.

It was almost bedtime. He had just time to see if the

big pieces of cardboard he'd picked up at C-Mart for the whale project were still in the garage. He ran outside. They were.

"What are you doing, Ollie?" Mom asked.

"Oh, nothing," Ollie answered. He came back into the family room.

Mom looked at Dad. "Haven't I heard that before?"

"Think before you act, Ollie," Dad warned.

"I have. I have," Ollie said, and left to go to bed before they could question him. Adults could always think of reasons not to do good projects. They could always spoil Ollie's good ideas. He would have to ask his dad if he could borrow his new camera, though.

After school the next day Ollie practically flew home. Bo ran to keep up, complaining the whole way. Getting out the cardboard, Ollie spread it on the garage floor. Mr. Dibbs hardly ever parked in the garage. It was too full, he said. Mom usually squeezed her little Datsun in, but she wasn't home yet.

With a huge pencil, the kind carpenters use, Ollie drew the outlines of two dinosaurs. He made them as big as the cardboard allowed. Then he lay down to check. Yes, they were as tall as he was. Fortunately, the cardboard came from refrigerator boxes, which were tall.

When Ollie was satisfied that the dinosaurs were the best he could draw, he traced the pencil lines with a black magic marker. Then came the hard part: cutting them out. He got the scissors used for cutting paper from the kitchen drawer and started to work. His hand got sore, and it took the rest of his playtime for Tuesday night, but he was pleased.

On Wednesday afternoon he went straight to the garage. There were cans of tempera on the paint shelf. Ollie had asked for tempera for his birthday last year. Washable paint always came in handy. His mom said she didn't mind buying him something that would wash off.

He got the biggest brush he could find and painted the Stegosaurus gray and the Tyrannosaurus rex brown. No one was sure what color dinosaurs were, so it didn't matter what colors he used, but he knew they weren't purple or red. Most colored illustrations he had seen made them gray or brown.

After the base color dried, Ollie added detail with black paint. Dolby watched, head between paws, glad the paint wasn't going on him this time.

"Hey, neat," said Bo, coming into the garage. "What are you going to do with those monsters?"

"Wait and see, Bo. It's going to be great."

"You always do neat things, Ollie."

Bo brought Alvin and Gary to see the dinosaurs. Ollie didn't mind anyone seeing them, but he didn't tell what he was making them for. A little mystery was good for business.

Rebecca came over on Thursday. "Hey, Ollie. You've done a good job. What are they for?"

"Wait and see, Rebecca, and save your money. You'll want one."

"One what?" Rebecca didn't like being left out of Ollie's fun, but Ollie didn't want to share his profits.

Rebecca was a big help, though. She steadied some scrap lumber while Ollie sawed it into pieces and made frames to brace the cutouts. Then she held the dinosaurs in place while he nailed the cardboard figures to the frames. So maybe he'd give her one photo free.

By early Saturday morning, he was open for business. Thank goodness the weather had stayed clear. He set the dinosaurs in front of the open garage door so that if the wind blew they'd be protected. Then he put up signs all over the neighborhood.

UNIQUE VALENTINE PHOTOS
GIFTS FOR PARENTS AND FRIENDS
3991 OAKWOOD STREET
ONLY $1.50 APIECE

Unique was his new word for the day. Just in time for his profitable venture.

On Friday, Ollie had asked his dad about borrowing the Polaroid camera. Mr. Dibbs thought about it for a minute and then said, "Sure, Ollie. It's a pretty simple camera, and the only way you can hurt it is to drop it."

Then Ollie had to tell his dad his idea since he'd have to ask him to advance money for film. He showed his dad the dinosaurs and stood behind one so his dad could see how it worked. He wished he could see himself. He had let Bo stand on a box behind Stegosaurus, though, and he thought Bo looked great.

Carefully, Ollie had cut off the dinosaur heads. When Bo stood behind the cutout, he looked like a Stegosaurus, especially when he growled. Bo smiling was too cute for such a huge beast. Ollie didn't know if dinosaurs growled, but the meat-eaters looked fierce, and surely they had big voices.

Mr. Dibbs told Ollie he'd buy three packs of film. Then Ollie could buy the packs from him as money came in. Any film Ollie didn't use, the family would keep for another time. The cost of the film made each picture run almost a dollar, so Ollie figured his price of a dollar fifty was reasonable.

Ollie set Dolby on an even bigger box behind the Tyrannosaurus rex. As hard as he tried, he couldn't get Dolby to bark or growl, so he finally took a photo of Dolby smiling. Behind the Stegosaurus Dolby cocked his head and put on his curious face just as Ollie clicked the shutter. When the pictures appeared like magic, neither dinosaur looked very fierce, but Ollie loved the poses. He taped them to a display board by the sign beside the garage. People would want to see how they'd look. He decided to take one of Bo as well.

"I look wonderful," Bo said, as the colors in the Polaroid appeared and the picture cleared.

Mom came out to see. "Ollie, that's a great idea. Oh, I have something to add to it. Just a minute. I'll be right back." She ran back inside. In a few minutes she reappeared with a big, heart-shaped candy box. Mr. Dibbs had given it to her the year before, and Mrs. Dibbs was

a saver like Ollie. They never knew when something might come in handy.

"Now, Howard, you stand behind that one." She pointed Mr. Dibbs toward Tyrannosaurus. She moved the Stegosaurus right up next to the other cutout. "I'll stand here." She got behind it.

Ollie had to step back farther to get both dinosaurs in the picture, but what he saw through the viewfinder was great. "Hold it upright so it shows better," he instructed his father.

Ollie and Bo laughed. Tyrannosaurus was handing Stegosaurus a valentine heart.

"Will you be my valentine, Steggy?" Mr. Dibbs said to his wife in an overly sweet voice.

Mom smiled, making her look just as pretty as Ollie remembered in the wedding pictures. "I'd love to, Rex, old boy."

Ollie snapped the picture. They crowded around to watch it come up. Alice came out to see what all the noise was about. If she insisted on a picture without paying, Ollie was going to lose too much of his profit.

"Hey, that's neat," she admitted, always skeptical of Ollie's ideas. All of them started to laugh at the funny romantic photo.

"Take one of Alice," Mom insisted, but added, "I'll pay for the family photos."

"Can I use them in the display?" Ollie asked, feeling better. "You can have them back tonight."

"Sure, Ollie," Mom said. "Good luck with your business." She went inside, but Ollie noticed that she peeked out occasionally to see who was coming over.

Alice insisted on taking her picture with her. Ollie grumbled but to his surprise, her wanting it paid off. Business started slowly, but about midmorning Alice appeared with several of her friends. They all giggled and posed, sometimes together, sometimes alone. He made twelve dollars from them, and they went off laughing, shuffling through their photos, talking about who they might give them to.

More surprising than Alice's crowd were the adults who stopped by. Gary's and Alvin's dads came over after each boy had his photograph taken. They had valentines made for their wives. Mr. Stenboom held the heart box so that it looked like he was handing it to Ollie. Of course, when he gave the photo to his wife, it would look like he was handing the candy to her.

Ollie noticed that the men liked standing behind the Tyrannosaurus rex. They liked looking fierce and growling. Something about stepping behind the dinosaur bodies made them forget they were adults. They laughed and giggled like teenagers. They growled and grimaced. Sometimes they had two or three pictures made to be sure they got a good one.

Soon Ollie couldn't even take time to count how much money he was making. His dad had to go get film for the camera twice.

Then something happened that almost spoiled the day for Ollie. A car pulled up in front of the garage. Miss Andrews got out. There was a guy with her, and they were holding hands.

8.

Ollie's Valentine Secret

"Hello, Ollie," said Miss Andrews. "This is my fiancé, Tim Huddleston. We were driving around when we passed Rebecca. I asked Tim to stop to say hi, and she told us to come over here and see your dinosaurs. What a cute idea."

"Let's have our pictures taken, Helen." Tim was the young man that Ollie had seen Miss Andrews with at the fur-seal rally in Denver last fall, the time Bo got lost.

Ollie couldn't tell Miss Andrews that he didn't want to take a picture of her and her boyfriend—soon to be husband. So he had to watch as Tim took her hand and led her behind the dinosaurs.

"You be Tyrannosaurus rex," Tim said. "You're always bossing me around."

"I am not, Timothy Huddleston. But Rex might remind you of who's going to be king in our household."

"Want to bet?"

The couple laughed and teased each other but finally posed, Stegosaurus handing Tyrannosaurus rex the red heart box, looking as if he was asking her to be his valentine.

Ollie had to pretend that they were just two of his neighbors. He stepped back until he could see both dinosaurs well and snapped the picture.

"Take two, Ollie," Tim called. "I know someone who will want a copy."

"Who?" Miss Andrews said, pretending to be jealous.

"My mother, that's who." Tim laughed and hugged the pretty teacher after they had finished posing.

They waited until the prints showed up, laughed in delight, and Tim handed Ollie three dollars. If it had been Miss Andrews by herself, Ollie wouldn't have charged her.

"Bye, Ollie. See you Monday," Miss Andrews called as they walked to the car hand in hand.

Ollie waved but looked away quickly as he saw Tim lean over and give a quick kiss to Miss Andrews. Teachers shouldn't be allowed to get married, he thought.

The day was almost ruined for Ollie, but he had to think of business and not his personal life. He kept taking photos until about four o'clock, when it started to get dark. He felt better when he found he had made twenty-five dollars. He'd work so hard for this campaign that Miss Andrews would have to be proud of him.

On Sunday afternoon Rebecca called Ollie. "Come over and work on valentines, Ollie."

"Valentine's Day is not for two weeks, Rebecca," Ollie reminded her. "I'm reading about dinosaurs."

"You've done nothing but read about dinosaurs for two weeks, Ollie. Come on over. Mother got me tons of supplies, and you can use all you want. Think of the money you'll save."

Rebecca knew Ollie wanted to save all of his newly earned cash for the dinosaur project. She knew how to tempt him. He didn't have to think long before he said yes.

"Okay, Rebecca. I guess I can read tonight. I'll come."

"Good. My father is making cookies, too, so we can have some hot from the oven."

Ollie hopped on his bike after loading a small backpack with some white paper, scissors, and paste. At the last minute he included a couple of his dinosaur books. Not that he thought he'd get bored at Rebecca's and have to read, but he might want to make some dinosaur valentines. He knew that the Chinese named each year after an animal. The year of the rat, the year of the dog, the year of the tiger. For him this looked as if it was going to be the year of the dinosaur.

Swinging around the corner of Oakwood, then Kalmia, he headed south on Nineteenth, pretending he was training for the big bicycle race Boulder had in the summer. He had to stop for the light at Iris, but on the next straightaway he got up some speed again. Cold air zinged past him. It was a gray day and overcast.

Maybe it would snow again. The weather report had said it might.

Ollie's bike made a *click, click, click* noise as he sped along. Maybe it was a rock in the tire. Then a different noise came from behind him. A kind of *ping, ping, ping.*

"Race you, Dibbs. Where are you going so fast?" Lester caught up with Ollie and started to pass him.

Ollie didn't want to tell Lester he was going to Rebecca's to make valentines. He knew Lester would make something of that. "Just around, Philpott. Why do you need to know?"

Lester turned off on a side street, made a tight circle, and came up behind Ollie again, pumping hard as if he was racing even if Ollie wasn't. As he flew ahead, Ollie zipped down Floral Way.

Phooey. Lester wheeled around and followed him. "You're going to Rebecca's, aren't you? Going to ask her to be your valentine, Dibbs? Oh, I love you, Rebecca. Will you be mine?"

"Shut up, Lester. You're just jealous because you can't even get a girl to look at you. It would scare her too much."

"Boo-hoo." Lester pretended to cry. Then he jumped the curb with his bike and skidded on Rebecca's sidewalk. "Oh, Rebecca," he called. "Are you home? Your sweet love, Ollie, is here."

Ollie ignored Lester as he should have done earlier. He leaned his bike on a porch post and rang Rebecca's doorbell.

Lester laughed when Rebecca opened the door. "Ollie

loves you, Rebecca. Better let him in before he freezes. Then you'd have to put your arms around him to thaw him out."

"Who turned you on, Philpott?" Rebecca hollered, and pulled Ollie inside. Then she laughed and took Ollie's down jacket.

The minute Ollie got inside, the sweet, spicy smell of cookies surrounded him. He was glad he had come. Mr. Sawyer was a good cook and an even better baker. He made all the Sawyers' bread and super cookies. "Hey, that's a good smell—hint, hint."

"Okay, we'll eat first." Rebecca led the way to the kitchen. "If we don't, we'll never get any work done."

"Hello, Ollie." Mr. Sawyer, wearing two big blue mittens, was pulling a cookie sheet from the oven. "You're just in time."

"I see that. You sure make good cookies, Mr. Sawyer." Ollie sat down at the kitchen table while Rebecca got two paper napkins and two glasses of milk.

Mr. Sawyer slid two steaming oatmeal cookies onto each napkin. "Tell me if you like these. I put currants and butterscotch chips in this batch."

The hot cookie melted in Ollie's mouth. Butterscotch crunched into the chewy oatmeal. He didn't even try to say anything but rolled his eyes in approval at Mr. Sawyer.

Mr. Sawyer laughed. "Does that mean yes?" He slid another sheet, covered with dabs of raw dough, into the hot oven and turned the timer to twelve minutes. Then he looked at Ollie again. "I'll bet you need one more before you can make a decision, don't you, Ollie?"

"I think so," Ollie agreed. "I'm close to deciding." He bit into a cooler cookie that was getting crunchy. "Yes, I believe I can honestly say these are the best oatmeal cookies I have ever eaten. I wish you'd give my dad your recipe. All he can cook is pizza."

"Maybe we can trade recipes. I've been looking for a good pizza recipe." Mr. Sawyer smiled and went back to filling another cookie sheet with dough.

Rebecca and Ollie finished their milk and went to make valentines. Rebecca's room was filled with stuffed animals—mostly bears. On one corner Rebecca and her mother had pasted a brown felt tree. Limbs spread out every which way and even ran onto the ceiling. Green felt leaves hung from the limbs. Some of the bears swung on swings from the tree. Others crouched on windowsills. Some of them wore costumes Rebecca had made.

"How can you *bear* your room, Rebecca?" Ollie teased.

"Easier than I can bear your jokes, Ollie."

They laughed and sat on the floor with paste, scissors, colored paper—mostly red—lacy paper doilies, magic markers, and a whole bunch of stickers stacked between them.

Ollie grabbed a sticker that read HIGHER AND HIGHER. It gave him his first idea. He drew a Brontosaurus lifting off in a hot-air balloon. With the magic marker he painted the balloon yellow and red and blue, since the dinosaur was brown.

"I'll Lift Off with You. How's that sound, Rebecca?" Ollie held up the valentine.

"Cute, Ollie." Rebecca fastened a big red heart to a paper doily. "Are you going to do all dinosaur valentines?"

"Sure. It's the year of the dinosaur." Ollie told Rebecca about Chinese new years.

About a half hour later, Peter and Frank came in. Rebecca had called them, too.

"I'm not a very good artist but I write good verses," Peter said, folding some white paper for his first card. "I'll trade some verses for some drawings."

"Fine with me," Frank said. "I'm much better at art."

"Is anyone giving Lester a valentine?" asked Frank.

"Maybe if it says, You Drive Me Buggy." Ollie started a verse. "This Brings You a Hug . . ."

"From a Slimy Slug." Peter finished the rhyme and they all laughed.

"Mother says I have to send one to each person in the room," Rebecca said, when no one had answered Frank's question.

"I used to have to do that." Peter rubbed out a word and chewed on his pencil eraser. "My mom doesn't pay any attention to valentines anymore."

"I wonder how it would feel to get valentines only because someone's mother made a guy send you one?" Ollie thought out loud.

"Awful," Rebecca answered. "But what can he expect?"

"Yeah, he brings it on himself." Frank waved a paper airplane. "He's such a nerd."

They changed the subject to the Stegosaurus campaign, and Ollie asked if they'd all be on the committee to testify.

"I'll make posters, Ollie, but I can't talk in front of a bunch of strangers," Frank said.

Pretty soon each of them had a handful of valentines and ideas for more. Ollie had a Brachiosaurus in a swamp. The message said, I'M SWAMPED WITH OFFERS, VALENTINE, BUT I'LL CHOOSE YOU. Another was Diplodocus, and the card said, I PLOD ALONG SLOWLY, BUT I'LL GET AROUND TO ASKING YOU TO BE MINE.

"How about this?" Peter got ready to read. "It's my best verse. Stegosaurus is on the front with a heart-shaped box of candy."

> I'm not too handsome
> with my plates bony,
> but my love for you
> is far from phony.

"That's great." Rebecca clapped. Ollie said he wished he had written it.

"I'm giving this one to Miss Andrews," Peter told Ollie. "You can use the verse on a card for your mother if you want to."

"Thanks," Ollie said. "I'll put it on the back of my Polaroid picture."

They talked about Ollie's successful photo sale, and

how he could use some of the money for the campaign. He tried out some new ideas on them.

"Time to break this up." Mrs. Sawyer appeared in the doorway with another plateful of cookies. "Come back soon, boys."

They thanked Mrs. Sawyer and Rebecca and left for home crunching cookies and leaving crumbs for birds. Ollie was glad not to see Lester on the way to his house, but he couldn't help but think about no one giving Lester a valentine. Or worse, only giving him a card because a mother had said to. He tried to remember that Lester brought it on himself. But then he remembered Miss Andrews's words: *You could be his friend, Ollie. Lester needs a friend.*

Ollie be Lester's friend? No way. He got home just as Mom and Bo were backing out the car. His mother rolled down the window. "Want to go to C-Mart before it closes, Ollie? Bo says he needs his valentines early enough to get them all written."

"Sure, Mom." Ollie rode his bike on into the open garage. Hanging his knapsack on the handlebars, he ran and hopped into the car.

"I'm going to get one for everyone in my class." Bo turned around and talked to Ollie until Mrs. Dibbs made him put on his seat belt. Ollie watched out the window as tiny flakes of snow began to fall. He tried to stop thinking about Lester.

"Let's hurry," said Mrs. Dibbs as they got out of the car at the C-Mart lot. "It's supposed to get bad fast."

Ollie looked at lots of valentine cards to get ideas.

72

Bo tried to decide between two packages. One held fifty small cards. The other had thirty bigger ones.

"You can make a few if thirty isn't enough, Bo."

"I'm not good at making cards, Ollie. I'd better get the big package in case I forgot someone or want to give someone two cards." He picked up the cellophane-wrapped box.

Mrs. Dibbs had gone to the back of the store for dishwasher soap and hand cream. Draped over one arm she carried a ten-pound package of birdseed.

"Can I borrow a dollar, Mom?" Ollie asked when she came toward them. "I'll pay you back when we get home."

"Sure, Ollie." Mrs. Dibbs got out a dollar and a dime and handed them to Ollie. "Including tax."

Bo looked at the big card Ollie held. "You're going to pay a dollar for one card? Who's it for, Ollie? Miss Andrews?"

"Maybe." Ollie kept quiet.

"Rebecca Sawyer?" Bo grinned.

"Maybe." Still Ollie kept quiet. And he would continue to keep his mouth shut for all of time. He'd decided on something he had to do, but he sure wasn't going to tell anyone.

9.

Lester's Trick

On Monday Miss Andrews had an announcement to make. "Class, Mrs. Ferrigan called me and said she introduced the dinosaur bill. It has gone through committee. We are invited to come down and testify for the senate on Friday. That gives us the rest of the week to prepare posters or signs and speeches for the senators."

Just this week? Ollie hoped he could be ready.

The weather stayed snowy and cold, so they stayed inside during recesses and worked. Frank was in charge of posters.

"Why doesn't each person wear a billboard like they used to do for advertising?" he suggested.

"Good idea," Sally Carstairs agreed. "We might also make paper flags of Colorado and put Stegosaurus on the flags."

"Some of the posters could be charts," Ollie said.

"Like one could list states that have fossils and what they are. That will be in our talk, but it's good to see it written, too."

"Or like in a fashion show." Brenda Hodges, who always dressed like a model in a fashion magazine, had on a felt skirt with a poodle on it. She got up and paraded around. "Ollie could say, 'California, saber-toothed tiger.' I'd have California on the front of my billboard, turn around, and the cat would be on the back poster."

"That would be more interesting than if we just stood there and talked," Peter agreed. "I like Brenda's idea."

So did Ollie. He, Peter, and Rebecca were still the only ones who volunteered to talk, but he liked the idea of not being up in front of a bunch of important people alone.

By Thursday afternoon the class was well organized. Ollie could hardly eat dinner that night, he was so excited.

"Are you really going to speak to the state senate, Ollie?" Alice asked.

"Not all alone." Ollie reminded Alice and himself so he could stop shaking.

"I'm impressed."

Mrs. Dibbs passed Ollie some more mashed potatoes. It was the only thing he'd been able to eat. Bo had made a river of the gravy, and it flowed off his potatoes. He wasn't eating, either.

"Stop playing with your food, Bo," Mom scolded. "Either eat or leave the table."

75

"I don't think I could get up in front of the senate and talk." Ollie's father wasn't having any trouble eating. He took seconds on pork roast, mashed potatoes, and the fried apples.

"Me, either," said Alice. "I told Bert Philpott about it. Lester hadn't even told Bert you all were going."

It sounded as if Alice liked Bert Philpott. If he was anything like Lester, Ollie thought he and Alice deserved each other. Tonight Alice had each fingernail painted a different color. Granted, each was a shade of pink, but it still looked weird.

Lester was going on the field trip, Ollie knew, but he hadn't volunteered to do anything. Miss Andrews would probably give him a job when they got there.

"Maybe Lester doesn't tell his brother everything," Ollie said. "But I wouldn't know. Lester and I are on *divergent* paths so we don't *converse* much."

Alice started to laugh. "I hope you don't talk that way at school, Ollie. People will think you're really weird, if they don't already."

Ollie gave Alice a dirty look. He liked to use his new words in sentences and in conversations if he could. That was the way he remembered them.

"People know lots of words they don't use in everyday conversations, Ollie," Mrs. Dibbs said. "So some of what Alice says is right, even though she didn't use a very loving tone of voice when she said it." Mom looked at Alice so Alice didn't dare make a face at Ollie.

"I don't think you're weird, Ollie," Bo said. "May I be excused from the table?"

77

Mrs. Dibbs looked at the plate of food Bo had pushed around, but not eaten. "Yes, Bo, but I think you'd better go on to bed. You're either catching something or you're too tired."

Bo went to bed without arguing, but Ollie stayed up until Mrs. Dibbs reminded him that it was bedtime, twice. In bed he tossed and wiggled for what seemed like hours. When he finally went to sleep and was dreaming of dinosaurs standing around in downtown Denver, Bo had a nightmare that woke both of them up. It was four A.M. Ollie groaned and pushed his damp pillow into a wad under his head. But when Mr. Dibbs came to check on Bo, Ollie pretended he was asleep.

The next morning he was tired and excited at the same time. Everyone in class was restless. The trip wasn't until the afternoon, so Miss Andrews finally gave up and read them extra chapters from *Wind in the Willows,* their after-lunch book. It was about a toad that had a motorcar, and it was pretty funny. When her voice got scratchy, Miss Andrews took out art paper. The paper had tiny squares all over it, making it easy to color a design.

Ollie became engrossed in his design and was finally able to relax. He jumped when Miss Andrews called his name.

"Ollie." Miss Andrews got his attention. "Will you go down to the office? It seems that Bo is sick."

Oh, no. Just what Ollie needed. But he left his crayons and hurried out of the classroom and down the hall. The nurse's room was just off the principal's. Bo sat there on the bed, eyes glazed, cheeks too red.

"I have a temperature, Ollie," Bo said. "I guess I have the flu."

"We called your mother, Ollie. She wants to speak to you." Mrs. Randall, the school nurse, was dialing the telephone as she talked. Ollie took the receiver and listened as it *burrrred.*

"Ollie, is that you?" His mother answered as if she had been waiting for Ollie's call. "Listen, I'm running these tests today, and I can't leave or we'll have to start collecting the data all over again. I can't get hold of your dad, and Alice has already left for lunch."

That figured. Alice's school had an open-lunch policy, and ninth-grade kids could go anyplace they liked. Alice always left the school campus because the rest of her friends did. They went to the downtown mall and messed around even if it was forty degrees below zero or there was ten feet of snow.

Ollie was beginning to feel squeezed in a big vise, and there was no way he was going to get out.

"I feel awful about this," Mom's voice went on. "I know today's your field trip, Ollie, but can you take Bo home? The nurse says he isn't too sick to walk. I've called Mrs. Rumwinkle, and she'll meet you at the house." Mrs. Rumwinkle had been their baby-sitter before Alice got old enough to be considered trustworthy. "The trouble is that she can't stay very long. I'll keep trying to get your dad. He might be able to come home in time."

And he might not. If he didn't . . .

Ollie looked at Bo, who was getting more glassy-eyed by the minute. His face was red all over now, and his body looked like a wilted plant.

"I guess so, Mom, but please, please, keep trying to find Dad. We don't leave until one o'clock."

"I will, Ollie. I promise I will."

Ollie told Bo to get his coat, and he went back to his classroom to tell Miss Andrews his problem.

"Oh, Ollie, this is terrible. We'll wait for you as long as we can."

"Rebecca and Peter have a copy of the whole presentation. They could read my part if I don't make it." At least Ollie knew the show would go on without him, but he wanted to go. This was the most important thing that had ever happened to him.

"Ollie, where are you going?" Rebecca stopped him when he grabbed his coat and hat. He took a minute to explain to her.

"This is awful, Ollie." Rebecca's eyes got big with sympathy and worry.

"I might get back," Ollie told her. "I'll do my best."

Ollie held Bo's hand and talked to him all the way home. He knew that Bo was really sick, and it wasn't Bo's fault. But why today? Tomorrow was Saturday. Why hadn't he waited one more day?

At home Ollie let Dolby in from the garage. Mrs. Rumwinkle put Bo to bed, and Ollie went back downstairs to stare at the clock. He'd left his lunch at school, but he didn't want it, anyway. He could never eat anything now. His stomach felt as if it housed an active anthill.

Dolby didn't know whether to stay upstairs with Bo or come down and look at Ollie. So he kept up a steady *pad, pad, pad,* up and down the stairs. Ollie sat on the bottom step and hugged the big dog every time he came down. Dolby sloshed his tongue over Ollie's cheek and ear.

"I know, Dolby. This is awful. Thanks for knowing that." Somehow Dolby always knew how Ollie was feeling. Ollie went in the kitchen to get Dolby some doggie treats and decided he could eat one banana.

Dolby barked, the front door clicked, and Ollie looked at his watch, all at the same time. His dad was home! And it was twelve-thirty. If he ran there might be time to get to school.

"I called a taxi from work," Mr. Dibbs said, shedding his hat and coat as he came in. "It should be here any minute, Ollie. Here's the money for the driver. Do you have your speech?"

He didn't. It was in his desk at school. But he might have time to get it or he could share Rebecca's or Peter's. Ollie tugged on his coat and went to the front window. Sure enough, a yellow car was coming slowly up Oak-wood, looking for the right number.

"Thanks, Dad." Ollie dashed out the door.

"Good luck," Mr. Dibbs called out behind him.

"Hurry, please," Ollie told the driver. "I have to go to the state capitol."

The young woman driving the cab looked at Ollie in surprise. "The dispatcher said Columbine School."

"Oh, yeah, I mean I have to get to the school in time to go with my class to the capitol in the school bus." Ollie rattled off the afternoon's events to the driver as they whipped up to the corner and down Nineteenth Street.

"Good luck," the young woman called as Ollie stuffed three dollars in her hand and ran.

The big yellow school bus was outside in the parking lot. Rebecca and Peter waved to Ollie.

"Come on, Ollie, I got your speech," Rebecca yelled.

"Dibbs—in—Place," Lester called from the back of the bus.

Ollie collapsed in a seat beside Peter and across the aisle from Rebecca.

"We didn't think you were going to make it, Ollie," Peter said.

"Me, either." Ollie took a deep breath. "My dad got me a taxi."

"You rode in a taxi by yourself?" Rebecca got Ollie's speech from her blue folder.

"Yeah," Ollie said. "It was neat."

The class was quiet going to Denver. They were all as nervous as Ollie, he figured. This was a big deal, going inside the capitol building and actually talking to the state senate.

The ride was both too fast and too slow. Ollie wanted to get there in a hurry and get this whole thing over with, but he needed time to relax, if he could, and to recover from almost missing the trip. Then he realized he had another need. In all the scurry to get Bo home and get back to school, he hadn't remembered to go to the bathroom. Now time and nerves worked together to make him know he couldn't wait all afternoon until their presentation was over.

When they got out of the bus, climbed the steps of the state capitol, and entered the huge building with the gold-covered dome, Ollie whispered to Peter where he was going. They were scheduled to meet in the senate room at two-thirty. Ollie figured he just had time if he hurried. He walked up the marble steps of the grand staircase to the second floor to see where the senate room was so he could find it again quickly. Then he took off.

A guard told him the bathrooms were in the basement. It was silly to have them so far away, thought Ollie. But he had no choice. He found a staircase and followed it down. The building was old, and he couldn't help but feel he was going to the dungeons. In the basement he had to ask one more time, but finally he found the door marked MEN and hurried in.

There was no one else in the room, and it was sort of creepy. The facilities were old, and the room smelled of pine disinfectant.

Automatically he tucked his speech under his arm and stopped to wash his hands. Then he grabbed a paper towel, glad he didn't have to wait for a machine

to blow hot air on his hands. Well, he wouldn't have waited. He'd have wiped them on his pants or waved them in the air on the way back upstairs.

Practically running, he turned and shoved at the bathroom door with his shoulder. *Thud.* He stopped short. His shoulder ached with the blow. Gently he pushed on the door again. It wouldn't open.

He was locked in the bathroom in the basement of the state capitol building. And upstairs the senate meeting was ready to start.

This couldn't be happening. He pushed on the door again. He hammered with his fists. But it was true. The door wouldn't budge.

10.

Revenge

Ollie stood, stunned by the situation. The door *couldn't* be locked. He had just opened it a couple of minutes earlier.

The radiator behind him rattled and thumped as if it were laughing at him. Otherwise, the bathroom was cold and empty. There was a window with frosted glass, so it wasn't dark. But where before Ollie had felt he was in a dungeon, now he felt he was locked in a cell.

He tried the door again. Then he knocked on it. He only succeeded in making his knuckles feel as bruised as his shoulder.

He felt stupid doing it, but he called out, "Help! Someone help me!" There was no sound outside or inside the small room except the slight echo of his words.

He looked at his watch. Two-thirty. He shoved at the door again. It was as solid as a steel door in a bank vault. Surely someone would need to come in soon. They'd see what the problem was and either be able to open the door or go get some help. He'd hear them and call out. He stood with his ear glued to the cold wood.

Minutes poured by like cold honey. Then they speeded up, making Ollie know that getting to the senate meeting was impossible. Two forty-five, two-fifty, three o'clock. They had only a half hour assigned to them.

Suddenly, to Ollie's surprise, the door opened and a man came in as if nothing had ever been wrong with the lock.

Ollie jumped. He had given up on opening the door himself. He leaned on a washbowl, his heart pounding. "How'd you do that?"

"Do what?" The man, silver haired and important looking, had on a dark gray suit and carried a briefcase.

"Open the door. It was locked or stuck."

The man went back to the door as if he didn't believe Ollie. He opened the door again easily.

Ollie didn't stop to explain. He pushed through it and ran down the hall and up the stairs.

Doors to the senate chambers opened, and Ollie's classmates came pouring out. Rebecca ran over to Ollie.

"Ollie, where were you? Miss Andrews waited as long as she could. Peter and I read your part."

Ollie felt as sick as Bo had looked earlier. He might as well have stayed home with him. It would have been less embarrassing than this. How could he tell Rebecca what had happened? She stood staring at him, waiting for some explanation.

"Ollie, they passed it! The senate passed it." Peter was as excited as Ollie had been, forgetting to ask Ollie what had happened to him while all the events were taking place. "They have to do the individual roll call on Monday, but it'll pass for sure and then move on to the legislature."

Miss Andrews came over to Ollie as kids started out ahead of her for the bus. "We waited as long as we could, Ollie. I'm sorry."

Ollie knew Miss Andrews was waiting for an explanation. So were Peter and Rebecca. "I . . . I got lost. Then I realized I was too late and I didn't want to interrupt you."

"Oh, Ollie." Rebecca sounded really disappointed with him. She turned and walked quickly toward the bus.

Peter turned to Ollie when Miss Andrews was out of hearing. "What happened, Ollie? I know you too well. You never get lost. Besides, how could you get lost just going up and down a couple of flights of stairs?"

Ollie checked to see if anyone was listening. Only Frank Ashburn, who had walked up still wearing a billboard that said VOTE FOR STEGGY. "I got locked in the bathroom. I know that seems impossible, but—"

"Hey, Dibbs, where were you? Lost—in—Space?" Lester grinned and sauntered by the three boys. He had a big grin on his face, the kind of grin that Ollie had seen before.

"Was Lester in the senate room when you started?" Ollie didn't want to believe what he was thinking.

"I don't know," Peter admitted. "I was too scared to notice anyone or anything. I didn't even see the giant chandelier until Frank pointed it out to me."

Frank thought for a minute. "Come to think of it, he wasn't, Ollie. After I relaxed I started looking around. I saw him come in when we were almost finished. A lot of people were standing over by the door, and he stood there with them, sort of melting into the crowd. He probably hoped Miss Andrews hadn't seen him come in late."

"Hey, Ollie, do you think that Lester locked you in the bathroom?" Peter realized what Ollie was thinking.

"I don't have any proof, but . . ." Ollie knew it. He just knew it. He didn't know how Lester had done it, but he had done it.

"You don't need any proof, Ollie. Isn't Lester always connected with trouble?" Frank said.

Ollie told the whole story again as they walked out to the bus, including where the man came in and said nothing was wrong with the door.

"Lester could have wedged it shut in some way until you gave up. Then he came on back upstairs. It was bad luck that no one came along earlier." Peter took Ollie's arm and led him to the back of the bus. Rebecca didn't even look at him as he passed her. She had sat beside Sally Carstairs. Ollie knew Rebecca was disappointed in him. He'd have to explain, embarrassing as it was.

"The way I see it, Ollie, we're going to have to get back at Lester," Frank whispered from the other side of Ollie on the wide backseat. "He's gone too far this time. Teasing is one thing. Even stealing the party clues was a prank. But this—this is serious."

"I wanted to testify." Ollie felt as empty as a balloon, wrinkled and out of air. He couldn't even get interested in revenge on Lester. Nothing could bring back the afternoon.

"It went really well." Peter tried to cheer Ollie. "And you wrote most of the speeches. You did a good job with the writing."

"Listen, Ollie. I have an idea," Frank said. "You leave this to me and Peter. We'll get Lester, and if anyone suspects you, you can have a good alibi. You can easily say, 'I don't know anything about it.' "

"What are you going to do?" Ollie asked. He sure didn't have any plan. He couldn't tell on Lester. And even if he wanted to do that, he didn't have any evidence. All he had was Lester's grin and realizing how good Lester felt. He just knew Lester wasn't celebrating the passage of the dinosaur bill. He could probably care less. Right now he was poking at Annie Wyatt and Mindy Hoffman. They were laughing and giggling for all they were worth at getting the attention.

"Don't ask, Ollie," Frank said again. "Then you really can say you don't know anything about it."

Ollie wasn't sure he liked not knowing what Frank had in mind, but he stopped pestering him to tell. Frank could keep a secret if he wanted to. He was much better at practical jokes and mischief than Ollie. He never looked guilty or embarrassed. He had what gamblers call a poker face.

When Ollie got home he found Bo fast asleep. Ollie's father asked how it went and Ollie said, "Fine." He couldn't say he didn't get to testify after all the trouble his dad had gone to, to get him there on time. He repeated the answer to his mom's question at the dinner table and if anyone wondered why he was so quiet, they didn't ask. Mom was concerned about Bo, and Alice wasn't even there. She was going to a party and spending the night with her girlfriends.

Ollie was so tired from not sleeping the night before that he went to bed early and fell asleep right away. It was a relief to escape all the events of the day.

Then before he could wonder what to do with Saturday, the phone rang and it was for him.

"Ollie, it's a girl," his dad teased.

Ollie grabbed the phone. It was Rebecca. "Ollie, I just talked to Peter. Why didn't you tell me Lester locked you in the bathroom?"

"Because I don't even know if Lester did it." Ollie retold the story but stuck to saying he didn't know what had happened. Not that he wanted to protect Lester, but he really didn't know, and he always tried to be fair.

"Who else would do such a thing?" Rebecca insisted. "I should have known you wouldn't get lost. I was just so disappointed. I'm sorry, Ollie."

"It's okay, Rebecca. Want to play Trivial Pursuit?"

Ollie had a junior version of the game that Alice had given him for Christmas. They'd played it a lot over vacation.

"Can't. My mom wants me to go shopping with her. I need new shoes. Maybe tomorrow. We've never decided on what to get Miss Andrews for a wedding present. I wanted to get something today."

"Go ahead. I'll think of something." Ollie wasn't interested in wedding presents. He found he wasn't interested in much of anything.

"I hope you're not getting sick, Ollie," Mrs. Dibbs said at lunch. "All we need is for the whole family to get the flu."

"I'm not," Ollie assured her. "I'm probably tired."

"Yes, you've surely had an exciting week," his mother agreed.

After lunch Mrs. Dibbs went upstairs to read to Bo. Alice still wasn't home. "Want to help me work on the car, Ollie?" Mr. Dibbs asked. "I think new sparks and an oil change will have it humming again."

"Sure," Ollie said. He wasn't much help as a mechanic, but he liked to watch and see if he could learn. He planned to ride his bike for a long time because it was better for the environment, but someday he'd probably have a car.

After hanging over the car engine or lying under it for a couple of hours, Mr. Dibbs said, "Hey, I'm hungry. What about you? Let's go down to Swensen's and have one of those huge sundaes. I need to go to the hardware store, anyway."

Ollie brightened. Suddenly he felt hungry again. He couldn't remember eating anything for the past two days. They asked Mrs. Dibbs if she wanted them to bring something back.

"I don't even want to hear the words 'ice cream.' I'm trying to lose five more pounds before spring clothes come in for real."

"Guess that means flowers instead of candy for Valentine's Day," Mr. Dibbs said to Ollie in the car.

"Maybe I should get Rebecca a small box of candy." Ollie was thinking out loud. "If you get a girl a present, Dad, does she get all silly?"

"Depends on what you mean by silly, Ollie." Mr. Dibbs turned toward C-Mart and Twenty-eighth Street. Swensen's was near the Crossroads Mall. "She'll know you like her."

"I do like her as a friend. I guess she'd get all silly. I'd better not."

They found a parking space right in front of the ice-cream parlor. Ollie ordered a Volcano and his dad decided on an Abominable Snowman. "We won't want any dinner and your mother will kill us." Mr. Dibbs picked the cherry off his sundae and ate it first.

"Yeah," Ollie agreed. He pushed the cherry to the bottom for last and dug into the marshmallow and chocolate syrup in the first layer. After a few bites he asked his dad about something else that was on his mind. "Did you ever have trouble with a bully when you were a kid, Dad?"

"We have a grown-up version of a bully in our office

right now, Ollie. That kind of person always causes a lot of headaches."

Ollie didn't know there were adult bullies. He hated to think he was going to have trouble with Lester all his life. Maybe Lester would join the navy and sail away to Africa or China when he got out of high school. If he ever did.

"Are you having trouble with someone, Ollie?" Mr. Dibbs started on the second layer of his sundae, slowing down a bit.

"Yeah, and I don't know what to do. Miss Andrews says I can either ignore him or try to be his friend. I don't think I can be his friend, and ignoring him has stopped working."

"There's no easy way to handle a person who enjoys pestering someone else, Ollie. But one thing to keep in mind is that bullies are nearly always unhappy people."

Was Lester unhappy? Ollie thought about that for a minute as he scraped into the last dip of chocolate ice cream covered with butterscotch syrup. Lester didn't have any close friends that Ollie could tell. He couldn't read very well, but he could do math. He had a paper route, so he probably had lots of money to spend. He had two older brothers, Bert, who was in ninth grade with Alice, and one in eleventh, who was going to join the navy when he graduated. Lester was always saying, "When Wally joins the navy . . ." They probably didn't pick on Lester since he was almost as big as Bert. Ollie came to no conclusions, but his dad's telling him that bullies were unhappy did him no good at all. He still had no clue as to what to do about Lester's tricks. And this last one was not funny. Not in the least.

Ollie and Mr. Dibbs stopped at C-Mart on the way home. Mr. Dibbs wanted to buy motor oil to replace the supply that he kept in the station wagon. Ollie wanted to look at his prairie-dog village. He always thought of it as his.

Mr. Dibbs also picked out a big, mushy valentine card for Mrs. Dibbs. "I figure I'll get a potted plant next weekend. Don't know where I'd hide it today."

They went in together on a Big Golden book about dogs for Bo since he'd probably be home from school for a week. Mrs. Dibbs said she didn't want him coughing forever like Alvin. Then Ollie settled on an extra valentine for Rebecca in addition to the one he'd made her. He'd just sign it "Guess who?" It had a polar bear on it and read I CAN'T BEAR IT IF YOU WON'T BE MY VALENTINE. She would know who had sent it.

He knew he should get Miss Andrews something for a wedding present but he didn't have any ideas, and he still didn't like thinking about it.

It snowed on Sunday, enough to be able to play fox and geese, a game of tag where you stomped out paths like the spokes of a wheel and the "fox" chased the "geese" up and down the paths. Rebecca, Frank, and Peter came over. They built a snowman where Bo could see it if he felt like getting up and looking out his window.

Then Mrs. Dibbs called to them. "Ollie, would your friends like to stay for supper? We have chili."

Ollie already knew what was for supper. Mom had been cooking it all day. It smelled wonderful every time they went in to get warm.

"Oh, boy, I'm starved, and I love chili." Rebecca went to call her mother. Peter and Frank agreed and followed her.

Mrs. Dibbs let them eat on trays in front of a roaring fire and then watch one early television show before they went home.

The weather stayed bad all week. Mrs. Dibbs started to talk about cabin fever. She had spent several days home with Bo. Mr. Dibbs talked about affording a vacation in Florida. But Ollie finished writing his dinosaur book and was almost finished with the pictures he'd drawn to illustrate it. He didn't mind some bad weather when he had a good indoor project.

Miss Andrews thought it had been a productive week. They'd moved ahead in some of their other work, and there was a long list of suggestions for the Stegosaurus project on the bulletin board. Peter had written an article for the school newspaper. Other students had wanted to help. Over fifty letters had been written and mailed from their own classroom, and the rest of the school had sent nearly two thousand. The letters went to students in other schools, authors, business people, and they told about the Stegosaurus bill. They urged people to write to the senate and the legislature.

Miss Andrews made assignments for the week she was going to be gone and made the class promise to keep working and not give the substitute teacher a bad time.

So on Friday everyone was in a party mood. The morning was devoted to oral reports and math games, the afternoon to art, and finally came the long-awaited valentine party.

The big mailbox on Miss Andrews's desk was decked out in red and white crepe paper. It bulged with valentines. The appointed mail persons started giving out cards right after second recess. The room mothers had made cupcakes with red icing, a heart-shaped sugar cookie for each student, and punch. Everyone got a box of candy message hearts from Miss Andrews.

YOU MUST BE CRAZY, one of Ollie's hearts read. When Lester wasn't looking, Ollie walked to the pencil sharpener and left the candy heart on Lester's desk. All week Frank and Peter had hinted of disaster to come for Lester, but Ollie hadn't seen anything happen. Maybe they were still thinking about what to do to get back at Lester, just in case he had locked Ollie in the bathroom.

Then about a half hour into the party, Ollie realized what the two boys had done.

"Didn't you get any mail, Lester?" Frank walked up the aisle and stopped at Lester's desk, covered with cupcake crumbs, but empty of white envelopes or colorful cards.

Ollie could see Lester's desk well enough to tell that all that was on it were chocolate crumbs, a soggy napkin

97

from punch spills, and three candy hearts leaning in the pencil slot.

Lester's face turned red. He gave Frank a dirty look and then started to clean out his desk. He heaped junk on top so it wouldn't be evident that he'd received no valentines.

Ollie knew that Rebecca had sent him one. Miss Andrews always gave each of her students a card, and Ollie had written "Guess who?" on one Bo had left over. Surely some other kids in the room had also given a card to every student.

But somehow Peter and Frank had gotten into the mailbox. They had taken out every card that was addressed to Lester. And today at the party, Lester wasn't going to get one single valentine.

11.

Ollie's Prize

If they wanted to get to Lester they'd found a good way. Lester kept digging in his desk and pulling out all sorts of junk. But his face got redder and redder. If Ollie hadn't known Lester so well, he'd swear that Lester was ready to cry.

The kids around Lester realized that something was going on. Rebecca looked at Ollie. He shrugged and tried to look away. Crumbs from his cupcake stuck in his throat. He went to the back of the room where the refreshment table was set up and asked for more punch. Mrs. Schultz, one of the room mothers, smiled and filled Ollie's cup.

Rebecca must not have been in on the trick. She didn't seem to realize what was happening.

Miss Andrews picked up on the whispering and the fact that one-third of the class was much too quiet. She circled the room and stopped by Lester's desk. She looked at Ollie, who looked away quickly.

"Spring cleaning early, Lester?" the teacher asked.

"Yeah." Lester ducked under his desk. He'd dropped his crayons and took a long time picking them up.

Delivery people kept making the rounds up and down the aisles with fistfuls of white envelopes and colorful cards. Ollie's desk was piled high. He had started to open them but now lost interest.

He wanted to feel great. Lester was getting just what he deserved. He'd spoiled many a day for Ollie. He'd ruined what could have been one of the best days of Ollie's life. He had at one time or another pestered almost every kid in the class. It was time someone got back at Lester. It was time something really bad happened to him.

Bullies are usually unhappy. Mr. Dibbs's words rattled around in Ollie's head until he felt like shaking it to get them out.

The room was suddenly too hot. Ollie tugged his sweater off over his head. But the hot feeling was coming from inside. It was as if he was being smothered in a huge cloud of steam.

There was one thing that Ollie could do. Fortunately he hadn't put the big dollar valentine in the box on Miss Andrews's desk. He still hadn't made a decision about the card that morning, convinced that he was being silly. Lester would get lots of cards and not all from people whose mothers had made them give everyone a valentine. Besides, Ollie had bought the card before the locked-bathroom episode. That morning he hadn't wanted to give it to Lester.

101

Now he slipped the card from his desk, where it was hidden in a dinosaur book. He bundled up his sweater as if he was taking it to the cloakroom. But he made a round trip, detouring by the big, open valentine box.

Fortunately, a sixth-grade delivery person had just brought a basket of ice cream from the school's kitchen. People were lining up to get a Dixie Cup and a little wooden spoon. No one was paying any attention to Ollie.

He made a successful drop-off, hung up his sweater, and got in line. Cherry ice cream sounded good. He took a cup, opened it, threw the lid in a trash can beside the table, and started back up the aisle to his desk, spooning in the sweet, cold treat.

Lester sat, still puttering with the junk from his desk as if nothing else was important. Ollie stood almost beside him when Sally Carstairs dropped the big envelope on Lester's desk. Lester sat staring at it for a second, then reached out slowly to pick it up.

Quickly Ollie passed on by and sat down. He didn't have to see the funny card. He didn't have to see Lester read FROM YOUR SECRET PAL. Knowing Lester had it was enough.

The party was soon over and bus kids ran to get their rides. Ollie gathered up his cards and half his candy hearts that he'd saved for Bo, still at home sick.

Miss Andrews stopped him before he could leave. "What happened to Lester's valentines, Ollie?"

Ollie looked at her, then looked away. "I don't know, Miss Andrews." He had lied. Peter and Frank had done what they had for Ollie. He sure couldn't tell on them.

Miss Andrews stood quietly, waiting in case Ollie wanted to say anything more. He didn't, so she gave up. "Thanks for helping Lester, Ollie."

She had seen him put the card in the box. He knew no kid was paying attention to him, but he hadn't spotted Miss Andrews watching. He had wanted it to be just his secret. But he guessed it wasn't spoiled because she knew.

He started to leave, not looking at her, not saying more. Then he turned back. "Miss Andrews?"

She had taken a seat at her desk and was looking at her cards. A present wrapped in wedding-bell-design paper perched on the corner. Ollie had seen Rebecca put it there for Miss Andrews. "Yes, Ollie?" She didn't look up.

"Have . . . have a good wedding."

"Thanks, Ollie. See you in a week." Her smile was as radiant as the sun, and Ollie felt warmed by it. He couldn't stop liking her, even if he tried. Maybe her getting married wasn't the worst thing that could happen. She could have moved away in the middle of the year. She could have stopped teaching.

Outside, Peter, Frank, and Rebecca waited for Ollie.

"Somebody spoiled it," Frank said. "But we really had him sweating, didn't we?"

Rebecca looked right at Ollie. "I figure it was Miss Andrews. Who else would see what was happening and give him a card at the last minute?"

The guys had told Rebecca the whole story.

"Yeah, Miss Andrews probably had some extra cards in her desk," Peter said. "But I'll bet Lester will stop being such a pest now. He was really scared, wasn't he?"

The friends kept talking about Lester and the party and Miss Andrews's wedding, but Ollie had stopped listening. He had learned one good thing today.

Lester was *his* problem. And he didn't want anyone handling his problems, fighting his battles for him ever again. He would take care of Lester himself, in his own way, in his own time. He was smarter than Lester. That had to count for something. And using his head would eventually work.

School was not nearly as much fun with Miss Andrews gone. And their substitute gave the class a chance to realize how lucky they were to have such a great teacher.

Monday morning a round little woman sat in Miss Andrews's chair. Her hair was bleached the color of straw and was done up in a beehive on top of her head. She was much older than Miss Andrews, at least fifty, Ollie thought. And there was not one grain of hope that she would play with them at recess or even sit and visit the way Miss Andrews sometimes did.

"My name is Miss Ironhorse," the substitute said. She picked up a piece of chalk in a tissue and wrote her name on the board in handwriting that looked as if it was Xeroxed from their penmanship books. "I have some desk work that I'm sure you will enjoy this morning." She picked up a stack of papers from her desk. "First we have a reading assignment. Review it carefully and answer the questions, and when you are finished you may start on the math problems. There will be no talking and no walking around without permission. Are there any questions?" She handed out a stack of papers to the first person in each row for them to pass back.

How can there be any questions when we haven't seen the papers yet? thought Ollie. He looked at Miss Ironhorse again. Even though it was February she wore a yellow tent dress that made her look like a balloon with legs. On her feet were plastic high-heeled sandals, and trapped in the plastic heels were flowers and jewels. Fake jewels, of course.

When the class settled down to work, she took out an emery board and began to file her nails. Ollie looked at her and she smiled. The smile made her huge butterfly glasses, the frames covered with sparkle dust, slide down her nose. She pushed them back with one long fingernail. Soon the smell of fingernail polish wafted down the aisles of the classroom. Rebecca looked at Ollie and rolled her eyes. She held out her hand and looked at her fingernails as if to see if they needed polishing.

Miss Andrews had made the class promise they would be nice to their substitute, so they tried. But by Thursday they were really bored by the busy work that kept them glued to their seats.

At first recess a shoe box mysteriously appeared on Miss Ironhorse's desk. The class got as quiet as a moon landscape must be.

A younger, more experienced substitute teacher would never have opened the box. But Miss Ironhorse probably thought that such a nice, cooperative class was incapable of playing a trick on her. She had complimented them over and over on how well behaved they were. She promised to leave Miss Andrews a wonderful note about them.

"Now, what is this?" Miss Ironhorse wondered in a small, quiet voice. "I can't think that someone has given me a present." She untied the red ribbon and carefully lifted the lid.

Not carefully enough. White mice ran everywhere. Over the desk they scampered, down the sides, tumbling to the floor unhurt, only to run across the floor seeking another shelter. The class screamed in delight. Six boys scampered to the rescue, gathering up the wiggling, pink-nosed rodents. And, to everyone's surprise, Miss Ironhorse helped in the capture efforts. Lifting each mouse by its naked tail, she placed it back in the shoe box, shutting the lid each time.

When all the mice were contained, Miss Ironhorse found two large rubber bands and secured the lid. Then she picked up the box and studied one end. She looked the class over carefully. Snow falling would have shattered the silence of the class.

"Mr. Philpott," she said finally. "Would I be correct in assuming that this is your property?"

Lester's smile dropped away and a puzzled look took its place. Quickly he looked all around as if she hadn't said his name.

"Yes, you, Mr. Philpott. That is your name, isn't it?" She knew it was. She had had to ask him to stop talking any number of times and had spoken to him on the playground twice.

Lester couldn't stand not knowing how Miss Ironhorse had so quickly figured out the box was his. "How . . . how did you know?"

Miss Ironhorse turned the shoe-box label to the class. "Size nine, large for most fifth-graders. And I happened to observe your new Nikes this morning. Elementary, my dear Lester. Elementary."

The class hooped with laughter, and a sheepish grin spread over Lester's face. He had underestimated his opponent and been soundly outsmarted.

The class gave credit where credit was due. They all thanked Lester at lunchtime for a much-needed diversion. Lester's smile lasted all day. Even though he had gotten into trouble, he seemed to think it had been worthwhile.

Ollie's new word that day was *shrewd,* meaning clever or sly. Miss Ironhorse had come up a notch in Ollie's opinion when she had outwitted Lester.

"Let's celebrate surviving this week by going to the mall Saturday, Ollie," Rebecca suggested. "We can collect signatures on the petition to elect Stegosaurus state fossil."

Their idea and their campaign had spread all over

the school. Besides writing letters, they had decided that collecting names to support the bill was one of the best things to do. And it was something other kids could help with. So Ollie and Peter had written up a petition stating support of the bill. They had copied the petition in large quantities. Half the kids in school had gotten the signatures of their friends and neighbors. Ollie had already mailed a lot of completed petitions to the capitol, aimed at the legislature, who still had to vote.

"Good idea, Rebecca. We can walk over. I'll come by your house to get you."

Bo was recovered from being sick and wanted to go to the mall with Ollie.

"We're working on our school project, Bo. Getting Stegosaurus elected state fossil." Ollie had kept Bo informed about the progress of the campaign while he was home sick. Bo had written his letter to the legislature at home. He drew a big picture to go with it.

"I want to help get Steggy elected, too," Bo said. "I can get people to sign the paper."

People would sign for Bo, Ollie knew. Bo was so cute that people liked to talk to him. Ollie wavered. He needed lots of signatures, but he didn't really want to take Bo along. He wanted to go with Rebecca.

His father saved him. "Bo, I need you to help me today. We'll clean the garage before spring yard work starts."

Bo was torn. He wanted to do both things. Mr. Dibbs

made chores fun. "Well, okay, Dad."

Ollie breathed a sigh of relief. He could just imagine Bo getting lost in the crowds at the mall. Dolby thumped his tail as Ollie started to leave. "You help clean the garage, Dolby. One time for you at the mall was enough." One disastrous time, Ollie remembered and smiled.

The mall was crowded as it usually was on Saturday morning. Most people were polite and took a minute to listen to Ollie and Rebecca tell of their project. To their surprise, Frank and Peter showed up, too, so they spread out, coming together occasionally to compare numbers.

There was a big sale, lots of giveaways all over the mall, inside the stores and out. As they wandered around stopping shoppers, all four of them signed up for stuff they could win.

"I'd like to win that bear." Rebecca showed Ollie a huge stuffed bear in the Noah's Ark toy shop.

Ollie could think of better things to win. He'd like one of the lighted globes in the travel store. Someday he was going to travel all over the world, looking at endangered animals. He'd find out what he could do to help them before they disappeared.

It was almost noon when they ran into Frank and Peter again.

"Look what I won, Ollie," Peter said. He held up a red baseball cap from a store that would put any saying or emblem you wanted on a hat or shirt. "I have an

IOU for a decal since I couldn't decide what to put on it."

"What about FAMOUS AUTHOR?" Ollie suggested.

"Then people will ask him what books he has written," Rebecca reminded him. "He'd be embarrassed to say none yet."

"Hey, I've got a great idea." Ollie started back up the mall toward the hat and shirt store. He pulled a billfold from his pocket and started counting dollar bills. He had this week's allowance and some of his Polaroid picture fund. Thinking he might want something to eat or who knows what, he'd put plenty of money in his pocket.

He looked at all the shirts hanging on lines outside the tiny shop. His friends followed him, curious to see what he had in mind.

"Can you really put anything on a shirt?" Ollie asked the young woman at the counter.

"As long as you can wear it in public." She grinned at Ollie.

"I want it to say STEGOSAURUS FOR STATE FOSSIL." Ollie ignored the salesgirl's teasing. She handed him a piece of paper and he printed the words the way he thought they'd look good on the shirt.

"Hey, neat, Ollie," Frank said. "I want one, too. How much will that cost?"

"Let's see. The shirt is five dollars. Twenty-five letters." She figured on a scrap of paper. "That would be seven-fifty."

Ollie had just enough money if he didn't eat lunch.

"I don't have enough," Frank said, after counting his money. "I'll treat for a piece of pizza, Ollie, and come back later. My mom will probably get it for me. I need some new T-shirts."

Rebecca and Peter said they'd get one, too.

"Maybe the whole class could sell them," Ollie suggested.

"My mom was talking about the PTA needing a moneymaking project the other night," Rebecca remembered. "I'll suggest it to her. I don't mind selling them, but it would be a lot of work ordering and getting them printed."

Ollie went into the little room where all the shirts and ink and stuff were stored and put on his new shirt after they'd watched it being printed. He'd gotten red with white letters and thought it looked neat.

"I'm hungry," Rebecca said. "Let's go eat something. Then we can stay longer. I don't have anything else to do."

The foursome went into Abo's Pizza, where you could order one slice and a soft drink. They sat at one of the tables, eating, when the loudspeaker sputtered on. It was an announcement of another sale and one lost kid. Then it announced a prize drawing, but the winner wasn't one of them.

"Oliver Dibbs," the speaker blared after they'd gone back to eating. "Another lucky winner. Come to The Peppercorn for your prize."

"Hey, Ollie, that's you." Rebecca squealed. "You've won something big. If it's the trip to Hawaii, can I go with you?"

"The Peppercorn. What do they have?" Ollie said. He had signed prize slips everywhere and stuffed them into boxes. He never thought he'd win anything, although he was usually pretty lucky.

"Who knows?" Peter said.

"Who cares?" Frank said. "It's free."

"Okay, what are we sitting here for? Let's go see." Ollie jumped up, stuffing the remainder of his pizza in his mouth and grabbing his orange drink to take along. He motioned for his friends to follow him.

Another lucky day!

12.

Stegosaurus Cookies

"Cooking lessons? I've won cooking lessons?" Ollie held the certificate from The Peppercorn Gourmet Goods and Cooking School. He hated to seem ungrateful, but cooking lessons weren't exactly what he needed. He had started to be less excited when they got to the store and he saw that it sold pots and pans and other cooking equipment, but Rebecca had said maybe he could give his prize to Miss Andrews. He could never give cooking lessons to Miss Andrews. Ollie was sure she already knew how to cook.

"Oh, Ollie, how funny," Rebecca said, now that Ollie had been handed the certificate. "You can give them to me."

"Boys cook," said Peter. "My dad doesn't but some men do."

"My dad's a great cookie baker," said Rebecca, "but I just can't see Ollie cooking."

"Okay, guys." Ollie resigned himself to yet another disappointment. How come things that *could* be great went wrong for him? "You're just jealous. And I'm not giving my prize to anyone. Unless . . ." Alice had a birthday in March. Maybe she'd like cooking lessons. Ollie tucked the certificate into his backpack.

The foursome gathered a few more signatures, but the crowd had started to thin. They were leaving the mall when Lester hollered at them. He hadn't been collecting signatures, just fooling around with his brother Bert and Bert's friends.

"Hey, Dibbs. What did you win? I heard your name."

"A hat." Ollie lied and snatched the red baseball cap from Peter's head. "I gave it to Peter since I have a lot of hats."

When Lester got past them Ollie said, "If anyone, *anyone,* tells Lester I won cooking lessons, I'll . . . I'll never speak to him—or her—again."

"We'd never do that, would we, guys?" Frank punched Ollie, and Peter grabbed back his hat. "No, never," Peter answered.

Good grief. All Ollie could do was laugh with them. Cooking lessons. Why him?

Miss Andrews came back to school on Monday. She didn't look any different. She didn't act any different. She said they didn't have to call her Mrs. Huddleston. Next year's class could do that. Things returned to normal. The class figured the whole school had collected thousands of signatures on the petitions that were then sent on to the legislators. They were feeling very positive about getting their bill passed.

The PTA loved the T-shirt moneymaking project. They had shirts printed in light blue and yellow. The shirts were printed not only with the message STEGO-SAURUS FOR STATE FOSSIL, but with a picture of a Stegosaurus as well. Ollie's mom bought him a blue one, and he took turns wearing it and the shirt he'd gotten printed at the mall. When the class went to visit the Denver Museum of Natural History they took one to the museum director. Miss Andrews appointed Nolan Schultz and three other class members to take a shirt to the governor. Ollie wanted to go, but Mrs. Schultz had said she'd drive, and Ollie knew he couldn't do everything.

Rebecca wrote a play about a dinosaur egg hatching after sixty-five million years of waiting. They performed it for the lower grades and invited Mrs. Ferrigan to come, too.

Frank directed the painting of a mural that they hung in the front hall of the school. Other classes made giant papier-mâché dinosaurs and decorated the school with them. Soon paintings hung outside almost every classroom. All of the school was in a dinosaur mood and backed Steggy's campaign.

Miss Andrews even thought up math story problems about dinosaurs. *If a Brachiosaurus weighs eighty-five tons, how many pounds is that?* Or: *A dinosaur went to Weight Watchers International. If he lost at the rate of 1,200 pounds a week for seven weeks and he had weighed*

160,000 pounds to start with, how much did he weigh when he finished his diet? A dinosaur on a diet. Ollie loved the idea.

The class got word that other schools in Colorado had sent dinosaur models, letters, and pictures to the senate and the legislature. Surely everyone there realized what an important event this would be. Colorado needed Stegosaurus for state fossil.

"Let's invite some of the legislators to our school for lunch," Ollie suggested. "Then they can see how our whole building is working for this bill."

"We can serve Stegosaurus cookies for dessert," Rebecca said. She looked at Ollie and grinned. "We have some very good cooks in our class. Maybe they can bake them so the school cooks won't have extra work."

"That's your idea, Rebecca," Ollie spoke quickly. "You'll have to do the baking."

Peter and Frank laughed at the joke that only the four shared. But after school they planned when to get together to bake the cookies. Ollie volunteered his house. How hard could baking cookies be? His new word that day was *culinary*. They'd have a culinary adventure.

"You can make cookies here, Ollie," his mother agreed, "but your father and I are going away for the weekend. We've had no time to ski, and if we don't plan this trip, winter will be gone."

"We're going to stay here alone?" Bo asked.

"I've thought and thought about that," Mrs. Dibbs said. "I decided you were old enough with Alice's supervision. But Mrs. Rumwinkle will be home if you need help. Also, Mrs. Stenboom said she'd check to see if you were doing all right."

Stay all weekend with Alice baby-sitting? Ugh. When Ollie weighed Alice against Mrs. Rumwinkle, though, he decided they'd have more freedom with Alice in charge.

So Saturday afternoon Ollie, Rebecca, Frank, and Peter gathered in the Dibbses' kitchen. Rebecca's mother had said they could come to their house, too, but they thought being at Ollie's with no adults would be more fun. Rebecca brought a sugar cookie recipe, and her mother had gone over the instructions with her.

"I'm not going to sit here and watch you make cookies," Alice declared. "Let me see the recipe." She looked at the book where Rebecca had a recipe marked. "The temperature is 375°." Alice turned on the oven. "Now, you just stick them in here for twelve minutes. Turn on the timer. You can call me if you have any problems. I'll be in my room."

Dolby didn't mind sitting and watching the cookie project. The problem was getting him to sit farther from the action.

"This is fun," said Frank. He had designed the cookie, drawing a picture of Stegosaurus for them to cut around.

"Can you make it bigger?" Ollie asked. "Like at least half the size of a sheet of notebook paper?"

"I guess so." Frank got out the supplies he'd brought.

He had cardboard and planned to cut out four patterns so they could each have one and work all at once. Cutting out the dough would take the most time.

"Yeah, that's better," Peter said, when they had the five-by-six-inch dinosaur pattern.

"I wish we could make them fat." Ollie kept thinking about ways to make the cookies better. They had invited ten legislators, and there were twenty-five students in their class. Making about forty cookies didn't seem hard, and he wanted them big.

"Mom puts yeast in bread to make it puff up. Why can't we put yeast in the cookie dough? It would make old Steggy swell up." Rebecca stirred four eggs into the cookie batter.

They all laughed. "Hey, good idea," Ollie agreed. He knew his mother made great yeasty sweet rolls when she had time. He went to the refrigerator and looked around for the yeast. Finally he found three packages on the door shelf. "How much?"

They had stirred up a double batch of the dough from the recipe while Frank was enlarging the patterns. Ollie looked at Rebecca. She shrugged. Neither Peter nor Frank had any idea.

"All of it?" Ollie guessed. "We can buy Mom some more." They had gotten money from the school Stegosaurus fund for the groceries.

"Sure," said Rebecca. "That only puts a little in each cookie."

By the time they got all the ingredients in, the dough

was hard to stir, so they removed the electric mixer and took turns stirring it by hand.

"Cooks have to be strong," Rebecca noticed, as she declared the dough stirred enough and dumped some of it out onto the counter.

"That's why Ollie would make a good cook." Peter rolled out the dough until it was flat.

"Well, you do have to beat a lot of things." Ollie laughed and flexed his muscles. He got out some table knives. Frank had the patterns ready, and they laid them on the dough and cut around each dinosaur. With a spatula they carefully lifted each cookie onto a sheet.

"Leave room for them to swell up a little," Rebecca advised.

"We have," Ollie answered. "Look, they're puffing out a little already. Let's bake two sheets at once. This will take all weekend if we don't."

"Hey, Ollie." Bo and Gary and Alvin came in. The day was snowy, the kitchen warm, and a house empty of parents appealed to everyone. "Smells good in here."

"Sure does." Alvin peeked through the glass in the oven door.

"Yum." Gary looked over his shoulder.

"When we make forty, *then* you can have one, Bo," Ollie told the boys. "But not before."

"Okay, okay. Can we watch TV?"

Mr. and Mrs. Dibbs didn't let the boys watch much television, but Ollie saw no harm in Bo and his friends watching on Saturday afternoon. "Sure," he said, knowing it would get them out of the kitchen. "And take Dolby with you."

Dolby hated to leave much more than the three boys did, but he had been scooting closer and closer until he was under the feet of the cookie bakers. Ollie told him he really did have to leave.

In just seconds, Bo hollered. "Hey, Ollie, come here. It's a show about tigers."

Ollie had worked before to save tigers in the wild. He had donated money to the save-the-tiger fund. He ran to peek at the show. Rebecca, Frank, and Peter followed.

"Hey, neat." Ollie sat down for just a minute. It was a mother and three cubs. They were going for their first swim.

"The little one is scared," Rebecca said.

"She'll push him in," Ollie said. "See if she doesn't."

"Tigers like water," Frank told them. "After they get used to it." He sat down next to Ollie.

Bo, Alvin, and Gary were on the living room couch. "Be right back," said Alvin, and ran out.

"Does she actually have to teach them to swim?" Peter asked.

"I don't think so." Rebecca sat on a footstool near the boys. The show was fascinating, the pictures great.

Alvin's voice and the funny smell reached them at the same time. "Ollie, I think you'd better come in the kitchen. There's a really neat mess in your oven."

13.

Choose Me, Ollie

The cookies! Ollie ran for the kitchen. Acrid smoke filled the air. Dolby started to bark. *Waaa, waaa,* the smoke alarm in the hall started to squall.

"Ollie!" Alice screamed. She pounded down the stairs. "What's going on? Where's the fire? We have to get out of the house. Everyone, *hurry!*"

By the time Alice got downstairs, Ollie had turned off the oven and opened both the oven door and the back door. He fanned the air with a magazine he'd grabbed from the coffee table in the family room. His eyes burned from the smoke, but finally it started to drift out, cold air taking its place.

"I guess we don't need to call the fire department after all," Bo said, disappointed.

"Of course not." All Ollie needed was for someone to call the fire department. He peered into the oven at the smoking mess. It *did* look like the leftovers from a fire.

The cookies had swelled up, run all over the cookie sheets, then over the edges and into the oven. Dough left on the sheets formed shapeless lumps. The bottom of the oven was filled with charred Stegosaurus puddles.

"It seemed like a good idea," said Rebecca, looking over his shoulder.

"It should have worked." Frank stood beside Rebecca.

"Maybe we put in too much yeast." Ollie didn't feel that anyone was to blame for the mess, but he sure didn't want to think about cleaning it up. And then there were over forty soon-to-be-ruined cookies to think about. Even if they watched them, they'd spread all over the cookie sheets before they'd bake.

"Alice?" Ollie started to say. "Will you—"

"No! I won't clean up this mess. It's your mess. You know the rule in this house. Whoever makes a mess cleans it up." She stood in the kitchen, hands on hips. She was ready to boss everyone around, but she wasn't going to help.

"I'll pay you." Ollie knew they had to make more cookies someplace and obviously not in the Dibbses' kitchen. And they needed to get started before it got any later in the day.

Alice thought a minute. "How much?"

"Five dollars," Ollie offered, knowing she'd probably hold out for more. She knew she had the upper hand since Ollie needed time to start a whole new batch of cookies.

"Ten," Alice said, her mouth set in a firm line. "And I won't tell Mom and Dad."

"That's blackmail," Ollie accused her.

"Call it what you like and take it or leave it. Cleaning an oven is the worst job in a kitchen without the burnt cookies."

"Okay." Ollie gave in. It took the rest of his money, but maybe it was worth it. He sure couldn't spend the rest of the day cleaning the oven.

"We won't tell, either, Ollie." Bo grinned. He and Alvin and Gary went back to the television set.

"I guess we can start all over again at my house, Ollie." Rebecca went to the phone to call her mother. "I feel like this is partly my fault."

"We all thought it would work." Peter took some of the responsibility, too.

Mrs. Sawyer said the bakers could come to Rebecca's house. The foursome confessed what had happened when they got there. Mr. Sawyer laughed, then said, "Let me see your pattern, Frank."

Frank handed him a piece of oily cardboard, one of their Stegosaurus patterns. Then he followed Mr. Sawyer to his shop in the basement. By the time Rebecca, Peter, and Ollie had the new cookie dough mixed, minus yeast, Frank and Mr. Sawyer returned with a metal pattern like a real cookie cutter. Mr. Sawyer had fashioned it from some scraps he had in his shop.

Stamping out the cookies was much faster than cutting around them. Mrs. Sawyer had suggested they use a recipe that made brown cookies, and soon the kitchen smelled like gingersnaps. Then she mixed white icing and showed them how to dribble it over the baked cookies for decoration, mostly eyes and scales. With all the help they soon turned out forty cookies for the lunch on Monday and extras for the bakers, even for Ollie to take to Bo and his friends.

"All's well that ends well?" Mr. Sawyer poured coffee for himself and his wife and milk for the cooks.

"I guess so," said Ollie, but he hated to think about what it had cost him.

Lunch at the school cafeteria went well. The legislators were impressed both with the cookies and the school's decorations.

"You can't believe how much mail we've received over this bill, Ollie," said Mrs. Norton. "Every student in this state seems to be interested."

Ollie felt proud. How could they fail with all the publicity they'd had, and all the letters the legislators were getting? He handed each of the legislators a dinosaur hunting license. They all laughed at the idea. Thinking about other people who would like them, he had already ordered more.

The license said the license holder could catch one Tyrannosaurus rex, one Diplodocus, two Stegosaurus, and four Pterodactyls, providing the dinosaurs didn't have any babies. But they had to take them out of the state within five days of shooting or catching them.

What a math problem. Ollie imagined loading a fifty-ton Diplodocus onto a pickup truck. He didn't know if you could even get it on a railroad car.

"I wonder how you prepare Pterodactyls?" Mrs. Norton asked.

"Baked like a turkey?" Mrs. Ferrigan suggested. She had come to the luncheon even though the senate had already passed the bill. She felt as if she was a key person in this campaign, since she had agreed to introduce it for the class.

Before they left, the legislators invited the class back to the state house to testify before the legislature when the Stegosaurus bill was introduced there.

"I wish we could do something really neat when we go back this time," said Rebecca. "Something besides just talk."

"Maybe we could take some papier-mâché dinosaurs along," Frank suggested. "They said they had gotten some in the mail."

"Then we should do something different," Ollie said. "Something no one else has done." Ollie was always looking for a better or a different idea.

"We can all wear our T-shirts." Brenda was wearing hers that day with her designer jeans. Usually she wore those shirts with the little alligators on them.

"We need to do that, anyway, in case the newspaper photographers are there," Ollie said. The class had been featured in the local Boulder newspaper and in two of the Denver papers the day Ollie missed out on testifying, and again when a reporter came to their class.

They were keeping a big scrapbook of all the publicity and the letters and things they did. Miss Andrews was always taking photos, and they added them to the book.

"Maybe we could make a movie about dinosaurs." Peter was still thinking of a new plan.

"That's a good idea, but it would take too long. I'll think of something." Ollie sat down to think of a good idea while the rest of the class made covers for their books. He would brainstorm every idea that came to him until he got one that was different.

Taking a clean sheet of paper, he put STEGOSAURUS IDEAS in the middle balloon. To loosen up his brain he filled in the space around it with ideas they'd already done. Then he started writing down new ideas.

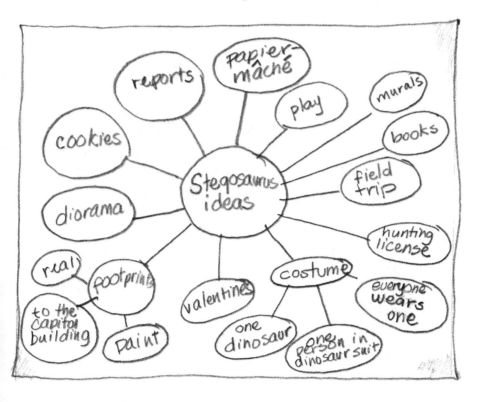

Wow! Ollie sat up and bounced his hand off his head. That was it! They could make a great dinosaur costume and choose one person to wear it. They'd take a person-sized Stegosaurus to the legislature. It would attract a lot of attention. The newspapers, even the television people, would love it.

They might use another idea he'd had, too. They could paint footsteps where the giant dinosaur walked. They'd have to get permission, but anyone who went to the capitol that week would see the footprints and remember.

Hey, this idea got better and better.

The class would love it. Ollie told them all the details after art was over. "The object is to get attention and publicity," Ollie explained. "The dinosaur would probably get his picture in every paper and on TV, too."

"Who will wear the costume?" asked Rebecca, after she volunteered to help make it. She was pretty good at sewing, having made so many costumes for her bears.

"Somebody big, I guess," Ronnie Swarts said in a disappointed voice. He knew that left him out. He was the smallest boy in the class, and people always teased him and called him shrimp and peewee and midget.

"Maybe one of our dads," Nolan suggested. "He'd look really big beside all of us. Who has the tallest dad?"

Before anyone could answer, Miss Andrews said, "I think it should be someone from our class. After all, this is our project. You can design the costume so the person in it looks bigger. That way anyone could wear it. The way you did the whale, Ollie." Miss Andrews reminded Ollie of a fall project he had headed up. The class had built the papier-mâché whale that was now in Ollie's garage. At least three students could fit inside. Ollie, Rebecca, and Frank had worn it during a save-the-seal rally.

"How can we decide who gets to wear the costume?" Rebecca asked. "Everyone will want to wear it."

"We can vote," said Frank.

"Then Ollie will get to do it. I know he'd win," Brenda Hodges said. "And he's getting to do too much."

"Then let's let Ollie choose," Miss Andrews suggested. "He thought of the idea."

"He'll choose himself," said Lester.

"No, we'll make that a rule." Miss Andrews smiled at Ollie. "He will be in charge of designing and making the costume, but he has to choose someone else to wear it, someone not even on the committee that makes it."

Ollie hadn't had time to think the idea through. He knew he'd like to wear the costume. He could see himself as Steggy, testifying to the legislature. His picture would be plastered all over every newspaper in the state and on every television channel. He would be famous statewide. DINO-DIBBS DOMINATES DINOSAUR DEMONSTRATION. STEGOSAURUS IS ELECTED STATE FOSSIL, THANKS TO THIS INGENIOUS BOY. *Ingenious* was his new calendar word.

"Okay, I'll choose," he said. "But only after we get the costume finished." At least that gave him some time to think about it. This would be special, a big honor.

They got to work, and Ollie tried to sign up some of the quieter people in the room to sew and paint. Frank would design the costume. Rebecca and three other girls volunteered to cut out the brown material, and anyone with free time could sew. It would take at least a week to make it.

"This is going to be neat," said Frank. "I'd like to wear it."

"Me, too," admitted Rebecca, "but I guess I'll have to testify again."

"You know I can't choose anyone who's my close friend, don't you, guys?" Ollie said one day as the foursome were working during recess.

"Yeah, we do," said Peter. "It's okay."

Everyone wanted to wear the costume, and they let Ollie know it. Some hinted. Some asked outright. Some even tried bribery. Ollie passed up a great bag of marbles, a package of new magic markers, and two dollars and seventeen cents. Maybe he should have made a choice as soon as they decided to make the Stegosaurus. Now it had become a big deal. And it looked as if he stood to lose a lot of friends, since he couldn't choose everyone.

"Choose me, Ollie," said Nolan Schultz. "Remember, I got the photographer out to cover your prairie-dog adventure."

Everyone reminded him of every favor they'd ever done for Ollie. Even Brenda Hodges, the best dresser in the class, wanted to wear the Stegosaurus costume. "Choose me, Ollie. I'm tall, and I wear everything well."

She had on fashion boots the day she asked Ollie three times. They made her taller than anyone in the class, even Lester. Ollie figured she'd worn them on purpose so she'd be taller.

"Miss Andrews," said Ollie, one day after school. "Maybe you'd better choose after all. Half the class is going to be mad if I don't pick them."

"Oh, they'll be good sports, Ollie. They'll go along with your choice. But if it's too much pressure on you, I will do it for you. I thought you'd want to be the one to say."

"Let me think about it some more," Ollie decided. But on the playground, before he could leave for home, three people hollered, "Choose me, Ollie. Choose me." Everyone had become his good friend.

That night he had a terrible nightmare. People were smothering him. They crowded him from all sides. "Choose me, choose me, choose me," they shouted in his ear.

Ollie shook himself awake. He had to make the announcement soon before it drove him crazy. But whom should he choose? Anyone could do it well. It wasn't a job that took talent or brains, speaking ability or artistic ability. But it had become a big deal. Everyone thought it was an honor to be chosen. And he was sure they knew they'd get their picture in the paper and on television.

He turned and tossed and turned. It was no use. He couldn't go back to sleep. He reached for the flashlight on his bedside table, then his journal. He kept it there because he never knew when he might get a great idea in the middle of the night, and he wouldn't want it to get away from him. More than once he'd thought he'd remember in the morning and he hadn't.

Who to be Stegosaurus? For a minute he thought about it really seriously. He visualized someone walking up the state capitol steps in the great costume. People applauded. Flashbulbs exploded. Under the covers, hiding the light so he wouldn't wake Bo, Ollie started to make a list.

One column said PEOPLE. Another said REASONS FOR. A third said REASONS AGAINST. He worked until he had the answer, and he couldn't keep a smile off his face. Tomorrow he'd make the announcement. He sure hoped he wouldn't lose too many friends.

14.

Lester for State Fossil

When Ollie woke in the night and made his decision, he thought he'd announce it on Monday. Then on Monday he had changed his mind. Now that *he* knew who it would be, he enjoyed the suspense of making the class wait to find out. People kept bugging him until they realized he wasn't going to tell.

"You might as well tell us," said Rebecca. "We can't be it and we won't tell."

"Yeah, we can keep a secret, Ollie." Peter and Frank had stayed in at recess with Ollie and Rebecca.

Ollie knew other people meant to keep a secret, but doing it was sometimes hard. He found it hard. And he knew the sooner he told, the sooner people would stop looking at him and smiling and waving and being friendly even when they didn't feel like it. So his secret felt warm and safe inside. He was enjoying it too much to tell.

All week at odd moments they worked on the Stego-saurus costume. It was going to be the greatest costume not only in the history of their school, but also in the history of all Boulder Halloweens. They used wire instead of wood for a frame so it would be lightweight. First they covered the wire frame with a big piece of brown cloth. Some scientists had pictured Stegosaurus as having spots, so with tempera paint they made light yellow splotches here and there. Rebecca cut out the bony plates that looked like giant leaves. Her mother helped her starch them very stiff, and when she brought the plates back to class, they sewed them on the back of the costume. For the spiked tail they made the brown cotton into horns and stuffed them with cotton.

The costume would fit over the wearer, who would have to have on a brown shirt and pants. The dinosaur's head was formed on top of a hood, but the wearer's face would be free so he could see. If he ducked his head down a little it would look like Steggy's head on a long neck.

After school on Friday, Lester, riding his bike, splashed water on them as Ollie walked Rebecca home. Big puddles stood everywhere from melting snow. "Going to choose your girlfriend, aren't you, Dibbs? Well, I guess there were girl dinosaurs."

"Lester the Pester-er," Rebecca hollered at him as she brushed off her coat. "What a nerd."

"I thought we were ignoring Lester." Ollie smiled at Rebecca, even as he brushed off his wet jean legs.

"Sometimes it's hard," Rebecca admitted. "And sometimes he's worse than other times. Even Miss Andrews got mad at him today. His dinosaur book is only just started."

Almost everyone had written and illustrated a book about dinosaurs and shared it with the rest of the class. In addition, students who wanted extra credit had written a fictional story about a dinosaur. Their unit would be over next week when they testified to the legislature. Of course, they would celebrate when the bill passed, electing Stegosaurus for state fossil, but that might not happen for weeks.

Saturday morning when Dolby brought the newspaper in, it was all wet and soggy. Lester was supposed to put a plastic wrapper over it when it was muddy or wet outside. For some reason he hadn't, and he'd thrown it into a puddle of melting snow. If Lester thought he'd bug Ollie with a wet newspaper, he was mistaken. Ollie didn't read the newspaper often. But Mrs. Dibbs liked her paper dry. She went straight to the phone.

"Lester," she said, after waiting for his brother Bert to find him. "My newspaper is so wet I can't read it. Will you bring me another one?"

Ollie knew if Lester didn't have an extra he'd have to bring his family's and his parents wouldn't like that. A paperboy had to buy more than one extra, and Lester probably didn't spend any money he didn't have to. Within half an hour, Lester had brought Mrs. Dibbs another paper. Ollie stayed out of sight. He didn't want Lester to think he'd had anything to do with this. And, of course, he hadn't.

But at noon Bo brought in the mail. There was a letter for Ollie that hadn't come through the post office.

Dear Oliver Fossil,
    You are the teacher's pet and a big trouble-maker. When you look for trouble you will find it.

The printing was sloppy and there was no signature. Bo peered over Ollie's shoulder as he read. They both knew who had sent it. "What are you going to do about Lester, Ollie?" Bo asked.

"Nothing." Ollie wadded up the letter and threw it in the trash.

But he found he was angry. He didn't like Lester's being able to make him angry. He went to his room and got out his journal. It was a good time to make another list. But this list was only to make him feel better.

THINGS I'D LIKE TO DO TO LESTER:
1. Send him into outer space.
2. Have the Body Snatchers come for him.
3. Invent a mud puddle that would splash on him all day long, no matter where he went.
4. Put him in a time machine set for 150 million years in the past.
5. Have the newspaper office deliver him five

thousand newspapers (Sunday edition) to
fold by five A.M.

6. Put him on a planet whose surface was a
foot of chewed gum.

Ollie was laughing by the time he finished his list
about Lester. It was almost as if he'd done all those
things to Lester, and he found he wasn't mad anymore.
He especially liked the time machine idea. He could
put Lester on the desert, surrounded by hostile Indians.
He could put him down in the middle of a Civil War
battle or during the San Francisco earthquake. He could
put him in a swamp where real dinosaurs would chase
him. It was much better than ignoring him.

He liked the planet of chewed gum, too. *Viscous*
wasn't on Ollie's word calendar yet, but he had used
his thesaurus to look up *sticky*. Then he found two
other words that he liked even better that meant sticky:
gummous and *mucilaginous*. Lester was up to his knees
in gummous gum.

All day long he thought of the list and every time
he started laughing. It was great fun.

By Monday he'd gone back to his original plan and
found he was still in favor of it. He had almost backed
out.

"Well, Ollie," Miss Andrews said first thing in the
afternoon. "It's time for your announcement. The costume is finished, and we're going to the legislature on
Wednesday. We need to finish our plans, and Stegosaurus needs to practice."

137

Everyone looked at Ollie, who stood up. Rebecca smiled. Brenda Hodges looked eager. She had bugged Ollie no end with reasons she'd be right for the part. Lester slumped in his desk, feet in the aisle as usual. He didn't look at Ollie, though. Ollie had never given him the satisfaction of saying he received the letter.

Imminence. His word for the day. Timely, he thought. His announcement was imminent. Anticipation was on everyone's face. He'd like to play out the suspense and attention he was getting a few minutes longer, but a glance at Miss Andrews told him she was losing patience with him.

"I . . ." He paused for dramatic effect. "I choose . . ." He paused again. People were on the edge of their chairs. "I choose Lester."

15.

We Can't Fail Now!

Ollie could have dropped a smoke bomb on the class and gotten the same response. Every face looking at him expressed astonishment.

Being Stegosaurus was an honor, the biggest prize of the year so far. And Ollie had chosen Lester? Lester was the most surprised of all. His mouth fell open, and he stared at Ollie as if he was in the time machine again and Ollie had just announced he'd been elected first president of the United States.

Miss Andrews's face held a huge smile, first for Ollie, then for Lester. "Excellent choice, Ollie. Lester will make a wonderful Stegosaurus. Let's see how the costume looks on him."

A smile started to take the place of surprise on Lester's face. Now that Miss Andrews had said it, it must be true. This was not some joke Ollie was playing on him to get back at him. Slowly he got up and stumbled to the front of the room. Miss Andrews lifted the costume off the double desk where it had been spread out for the weekend.

Frank whispered to Ollie. "That's the dumbest thing you've ever done, Dibbs. Why did you choose Lester?"

Ollie didn't think Frank really expected an answer to his question. And he wasn't sure he could give one.

He had done a lot of thinking about Lester that night he couldn't sleep. He had tried to think of why Lester acted the way he did. The obvious reason was that he had trouble reading and people thought he was dumb. Maybe even Lester thought himself dumb. Ollie knew he wasn't. He could do math. He had a successful paper route.

Ollie wanted someone big for the Stegosaurus. Lester was the biggest kid in class. And Ollie figured that probably made Lester unhappy, too. Lester stood out from the other fifth-graders in the class like a dinosaur in a crowd of iguanas. Everyone teased Ronnie Swarts over being the smallest kid in class. No one dared tease Lester for being the biggest. Lester would kill anyone who did. But Lester's size was just as obvious as Ronnie's, maybe even more so.

Ollie figured that Lester needed to be Stegosaurus. And, besides, he'd be good at it. Maybe no one else in the whole class would understand Ollie's choice, but Ollie didn't care. He had figured out what to do about Lester. And he felt good about it.

When Lester got the costume on, he paraded around the classroom. Ollie was right. Lester was perfect for the part. Lester as Steggy looked important. He'd stand out in any crowd.

"I think Lester should parade around the whole school at recess," Rebecca said. "He can carry one of our signs and everyone in school can see our costume."

"Good idea, Rebecca," Miss Andrews agreed.

Other people in the class carried signs and posters and paraded with Lester. Ollie asked Ronnie if he'd hold up the Stegosaurus tail to keep it out of the mud puddles, but he himself didn't go with the class. Most of them had taken Ollie's choice good-naturedly after the shock had worn off, and they joined the parade.

"That was a very good idea, Ollie," Rebecca said to him as they watched the parade leave. "You know what, Ollie? I like you."

"Good grief, Rebecca." Ollie pretended to be disgusted by Rebecca's confession. But, to tell the truth, he felt pretty good because Rebecca had said it. Maybe Frank and Peter didn't understand about Stegosaurus and Lester, but Rebecca did.

At home, Ollie found Bo didn't understand, either. "Why did you choose Lester to be Steggy, Ollie? Lester's not your friend."

"Because he'll be good at being Steggy, Bo," Ollie said, not even trying to explain.

Wednesday came almost too fast. Ollie was even more nervous because he'd missed out the first time they testified. Rebecca and Peter were calm since they'd done it before, so Ollie tried to stop wiggling in his seat on the bus, whizzing along the turnpike to Denver.

"Lester looks pretty good," Peter admitted when they gathered in front of the big building with the gold dome. It was the first week of March and one of those days that hints of spring when you know the real warm weather is a month or two away. Rocky Mountain springs were snowier than winters.

Lester had on brown corduroy pants—new ones his mom had bought him, a brown sweatshirt, and brown moon boots. Rebecca wanted to make dinosaur boots, but she couldn't figure out how.

They'd settled for the moon boots, which were big and made a person's feet and ankles look like elephant feet.

Miss Andrews had gotten permission for them to paint dinosaur footprints on the sidewalk leading up to the capitol and up the steps. They had to use washable paint, but with any luck with the weather the footprints would last a few days. Behind Lester walked three kids, two holding the pattern with a cutout footprint and one carrying a plastic bucket of white tempera paint.

Ollie looked back from the top of the long flight of steps. The footprints looked really neat.

Lester strutted for the television cameras that were filming this last visit of the class. Maybe someone had tipped them off as to something special this trip. Ollie tried not to feel jealous that Lester was getting all the attention. Then Miss Andrews had Peter, Rebecca, and Ollie speak to a reporter, telling him about the project.

Their interview was filmed, too, and they could watch it on television that very evening, the reporter told them.

The legislators listened carefully as Peter told the background of Stegosaurus in Colorado. Rebecca shared her list of other states having state fossils. And Ollie told them why Stegosaurus should be elected state fossil of Colorado. Others in the class paraded by with their posters and billboards as the three spoke, and soon many were lined up in front of the room.

Ollie held his breath as the speaker of the house asked for a first voice vote on the bill. Everyone said yes. The first step was finished. Two more votes in the legislature and the bill would go to the governor for signing. Then it would be a law. It was happening. Their law was being passed.

Back in the bus everyone cheered. They were noisy all the way home, but Miss Andrews didn't tell them to be quiet once.

Then a week later their luck changed.

"Class." Miss Andrews asked for their attention before dismissal on Thursday. "I have some bad news— not all bad, but disappointing. The legislators recessed before they got to our bill again. So it won't be passed this spring."

"That's not fair," Ollie said aloud, thinking he was talking to himself. "That's just not fair."

16.

Ollie Saves the Day

Friday was a half day so teachers could meet with parents and give them good news or bad news about their kids. Ollie had worried all evening and half the night about the Stegosaurus bill. He found some of the rest of the class had, too. At first recess they gathered around Ollie.

"What are you going to do, Ollie?" Brenda Hodges asked.

"*We* do, Brenda. What are *we* going to do." Ollie noticed when an idea didn't work out people remembered it was his idea again.

"Well, have another good idea, Ollie." Ronnie Swarts stood on the outside of the circle around Ollie. He pushed forward to talk to him.

Even Lester stood nearby, not part of the group, but listening. He hadn't said anything to Ollie about being chosen Stegosaurus. Ollie didn't expect him to, and he wasn't sure he wanted Lester to say anything. He knew he and Lester could never be friends. All he wanted was for Lester to stop bugging him.

"Good ideas aren't floating around out here like germs, Ronnie," Ollie reminded him.

"There's only one thing left to do," Rebecca said, and everyone turned to listen to her. Ollie didn't even mind her taking away his spotlight. Sometimes he was glad for people to ignore him.

"What's that?" asked Peter.

"I think Ollie should call up the governor and tell him our problem. He was interested and he liked the shirt. He knew what we were trying to do."

"I can't just call up the governor of the state of Colorado." Ollie had hoped for a sensible solution to their problem.

"Why not?" asked Rebecca. "Other people do."

"Well . . . well . . . they probably wouldn't let me talk to him." Ollie wasn't sure who "they" were, but he didn't figure you could call the governor and he'd say hello like when Ollie called Peter or Rebecca. Even when Ollie called his mom at work, her secretary would say, "I'll see if she can talk to you."

The governor's secretary would say, "I'm sorry, he's busy," or "I'm sorry, he doesn't have time to talk to kids."

"It's worth a try, Ollie," said Frank. "We did all this work. We can't quit now."

"Yeah," Peter added. "Maybe they'll get around to

passing the bill in the fall, or someday, but what fun is that?"

"We know you can do it, Ollie," Brenda said. She had stopped wearing her fashion boots to make her look taller; now she had on expensive pink tennis shoes to match her pink skirt and fuzzy sweater.

"What's the worst thing that could happen?" Peter said. "He'd have someone say he was too busy to talk or he'd say he couldn't help us."

Put that way, Ollie could think of no other reason to refuse to call except that the idea of it made him feel as if corn was popping in his stomach.

Five people went home with him at noon. Rebecca, Frank, Peter, Brenda, and Nolan. They called their parents to say where they were going to be for the afternoon.

Mrs. Dibbs had taken the afternoon off for her conference with Miss Andrews, but her appointment wasn't until two-thirty. "What is this, Ollie? A party?"

Ollie could see she wasn't angry when she opened two more cans of vegetable soup.

"I guess you could call us a support group." Rebecca laughed. "My mother is trying to stop smoking, and she has people she calls for encouragement. They meet together sometimes to talk about how hard it is. We're here to support Ollie while he calls the governor."

Support, Ollie thought. More like hold me up.

"You're calling the governor, Ollie?" Mrs. Dibbs paused, soup can in hand. "The governor of Colorado?"

"Hey, you could call the governor of Wyoming, too," Nolan suggested. "Have him call our governor and tell him having a state fossil is a good idea."

"Don't worry, Mom," Ollie assured her. "I'm not going to run up the phone bill."

Dolby usually lay under Ollie's feet when they ate. There was a rule about not feeding him at the table, but he was there in case someone was messy. He got so excited about having so many possibly messy kids there, Mrs. Dibbs had to put him outside.

"Poor Dolby." Bo crumbled crackers in his soup. "He thought it was a party."

"This is scary." Ollie had started to shake so much that when they finished lunch Peter had to look through the phone book to get the phone number at the capitol. The letters from his alphabet soup formed the word *panic* in his stomach.

"Pretend you're calling Mr. Hawkins," Brenda suggested. She sat on the couch in the family room and smoothed her pink circle skirt around her.

"I never call the principal." Ollie wondered if he could suddenly lose his voice. This was even worse because seven people and one dog (Dolby had barked until Mrs. Dibbs gave up and let him back in) sat watching him dial. He had asked his mother to talk first, but she said *she* didn't have the nerve to call the governor.

Ollie took a deep breath while he listened to the phone ringing at the capitol building. "Hello," he said when a voice answered, "State capitol." "I would like to speak to . . . to"—Ollie swallowed the lump in his throat—"to the governor."

"May I say who's calling, please?" The voice was friendly.

"My name is Oliver Dibbs and I'm calling about the Stegosaurus bill." It sounded important to say he wanted to talk about a bill.

"One moment, please."

Never had one moment seemed so long. Ollie felt he could have ridden his bike to C-Mart and back.

A deep voice came on the line. "Hello, Oliver. What can I do for you?"

Just like that? So easy? What can I do for you?

"Uh . . . uh . . ." Ollie was speechless.

Quickly Rebecca printed in big letters on a page from her notebook: *I'm calling about the Stegosaurus bill.*

Ollie read and found his voice. "It's about the Stegosaurus bill, sir." It seemed like a good idea to say sir. "You see, the legislators went to recess before they could pass it, and we've worked for two months and . . ." Ollie told the governor the whole story and how his class felt and even got around to saying it didn't seem fair for them to have to wait until fall.

"I'll look into this, Oliver. There might be something I can do. And thank you for calling. I always like to talk to the people in my state."

"You do?" Ollie hated it that he sounded so surprised.

"I certainly do. I'll call you back as soon as I can."

Ollie hung up and sat frozen for a minute.

"Oh, Ollie," Rebecca teased. "You said the legislators

went *to* recess instead of on recess. You made them sound like fifth-graders."

Everyone started to laugh. "I did?" Ollie started laughing, too, partly because of his mistake and partly because he felt so good. He told everyone what the governor had said. "At least we tried," he reminded them all.

"This calls for a celebration," Mrs. Dibbs said, getting up to get ready for her conference. "If all of you can stay, I'll stop for ice cream on the way back."

"Can I invite Alvin and Gary?" Bo took off to get them without waiting for an answer.

"Let's play Trivial Pursuit," Peter suggested. He remembered that Ollie had a junior game.

The support group turned into a party. Everyone felt better because they had done something, or had gotten Ollie to do it.

It was almost noon on Monday when an announcement came over the intercom in Ollie's fifth-grade classroom. "Would Oliver Dibbs please come to the office. He has a phone call from the governor."

Ollie sat glued to his desk until three people pushed at him.

"Ollie, go on." Frank poked him again.

Ollie ran to the office and then was too out of breath to talk. He gulped in breaths of air before he took the call in Mr. Hawkins's office.

"Oliver? Is this Oliver Dibbs?" It was the same friendly voice.

"Yes, I think so," Ollie stammered. "I mean . . ." What a dumb thing to say. "Yes, hello." He started again. "This is Oliver Dibbs."

"I feel sure the legislature will pass the Stegosaurus bill in the fall, Oliver. But I realize that seems a long time off to you. So, meanwhile, I've decided to declare Stegosaurus state fossil."

"Can you do that?" Another dumb remark. The governor could do anything he liked in the state, Ollie figured.

"Yes, I can, Oliver. How would you feel about my coming to your school next week to make it official?"

"Wow!" Ollie nearly shouted into the phone. "Wow, sir," he said in a quieter voice. "That would be great. My class would be really happy."

"I'm glad I can help out. I like this idea, Oliver. And your school has worked hard. If you'll put someone there on the line, my secretary will work out the details with him."

Ollie handed the phone to Mr. Hawkins. He and the secretary and two teachers on coffee break had been standing in the doorway.

Ollie ran all the way back to his room and then couldn't speak again. Finally he told Miss Andrews and the class what the governor had said. Everyone cheered.

"There should be an assembly." Miss Andrews started to plan the occasion.

"We should declare it Stegosaurus Day," Ollie suggested.

New ideas flew back and forth so quickly that it took

them a half hour to calm down and make some serious plans.

By the time Stegosaurus Day finally arrived, Ollie hadn't slept for three days. His breakfast oatmeal landed in his stomach like a bowlful of papier-mâché. He hadn't heard a word Bo had said on the way to school, and Bo chattered nonstop. He was excited, too. The whole school was excited.

Miss Andrews gave up and declared it a Friday. They did math games and a spelling bee all morning. Almost no one ate lunch, and spaghetti was on the menu. This time the school cooks made dinosaur cookies. Ollie nibbled on the sugary treat but hardly tasted it.

Everyone who had a Stegosaurus T-shirt wore it. Ollie was disappointed that the governor didn't wear his. But he probably figured that a coat and tie looked better on television. The all-purpose room was full of television cameras and reporters.

All their class was up in front of the whole school. They had dressed Lester in the Stegosaurus costume and decorated the room with art projects. The school had been covered with dinosaur art for weeks. Dinosaurs hung from the ceiling and marched around the walls.

Ollie introduced the governor. He told Miss Andrews she should do that, but she said no, it was Ollie's job. So Ollie stood in front of the whole school until everyone was quiet.

"Fellow classmates," he said. He thought that sounded funny, but he didn't want to say "Boys and girls" or "Listen, you guys." "All of you know how hard we've worked for the Stegosaurus bill and why we're here today. So without further words from me, I'd like to introduce the governor of the state of Colorado."

Everyone cheered, and it took five minutes for them to get quiet again. "I'm glad to be here today," the governor said. Then he read his proclamation. When he got to the part that said, "I officially declare Stego-saurus state fossil," the room sounded like two dozen trains roaring at once. Two hundred kids cheered for Stegosaurus and the governor. Television cameras whirred.

Two reporters asked Ollie to stand by the governor while they took more photos. "I think Stegosaurus should stand up here, too," said Ollie, and motioned for Lester to come get in the picture.

The reporters loved it, and pretty soon Ollie's face felt frozen in a smile. But he kept smiling all the same.

"This is my brother," Bo said to a reporter. Ollie wondered how long he had been standing there.

Back in the room Miss Andrews surprised them with a party. Ollie realized he was starving. Now he wanted his spaghetti, not cake and lemonade, not even a cake shaped like Stegosaurus. While they ate Ollie handed around dinosaur hunting licenses he'd made out for everyone. As he gave the license, he said thank you to every class member. Lester took his and quickly looked away, but Ollie said thank you, anyway. Then he added, "You were a great Stegosaurus, Lester."

DINOSAUR HUNTING LICENSE
. . . good for . . .

1 Tyrannosaurus rex   2 Stegosaurus
1 Diplodocus   4 Pterodactyls

. . . providing . . .

• they do not have babies
• you take them out of the state within 5 days of shooting or catching

_____

Chamber of Commerce, Vernal, Utah

As they started home on their bikes, Rebecca said, "Boy, the rest of the year is going to be boring."

"Maybe not." Ollie figured Rebecca was right, but he didn't want to think so. But what could top the dinosaur cause?

He was a block from home when Lester sped by him. Lester circled around, popped a wheelie, then circled again, coming up behind Ollie. Ollie kept riding along as if Lester wasn't there.

"Dibbs?" Lester spoke in such a quiet voice that Ollie could hardly hear him. He rode up beside Ollie.

155

"Yes?" Ollie looked at Lester. He was all in brown, and his moon boots swallowed up his bike pedals.

"Thanks, Dibbs." Lester stood up, pedaling hard, and sped off again, leaving Ollie to wonder if he'd heard right. Lester had actually said thanks?

Bo ran up behind Ollie as Ollie put his bike in the garage. "What did Lester say to you, Ollie?" Bo had been walking with Alvin and Gary.

"Oh, nothing," Ollie said. "I'm hungry. Let's go see what's for snacks."

Ollie, Bo, and Alice watched "First News" at four-thirty on the television. Mr. and Mrs. Dibbs joined them for the five-thirty and the six-thirty local news. The school event was on all three times. During the first program Ollie looked at himself, standing beside the governor. The next two times he looked at Lester as Stegosaurus. He had never seen such a big smile on Lester's face. And it wasn't the usual pestering Lester grin. It was a real smile. A happy smile.

"Wow, you're famous again, Ollie," Bo said. "Really famous."

It was funny. Ollie knew he should feel great when Bo said he was famous. But he found he didn't even care. All he cared about was the smile on Lester's face, seeing Lester look happy. It made Ollie have a nice warm feeling inside. And the warm spot felt as if it would stay with him for a long time. Maybe even until Lester graduated from high school, joined the navy, and sailed off to some distant planet all his own.